AF444593

Old Man's Journey

A Modern-Day Fairy Tale

Robert A. Pauker

Robert Pauker is available to speak at selected engagements. If you are interested, contact him at c3pauker@gmail.com. (Be sure to indicate "speaking engagement" in the subject line.)

Old Man's Journey: A Modern-Day Fairy Tale is a work of fiction. Names, characters, places, businesses, events and incidents are the products of the author's imagination or are used fictitiously. Any resemblance to actual persons, living or dead, or actual events is purely coincidental.

Old Man's Journey: A Modern-Day Fairy Tale
Copyright © 2022 Robert A. Pauker All rights reserved.

ISBN: 9798814526243

No part of this publication may be reproduced or distributed in any form or by any means, or stored in a database or retrieval system, without the prior written permission of the author.

Table of Contents

For
Andrew and Ben
and
Ben and Andrew

Introduction

I first visualized Old Man in the spring of 2014. Between March and December of 2014, I wrote a first draft of this book. I immediately saw Old Man as a kind, but vulnerable spirit who destroyed what could have been a rather normal, successful life. His mind cannot let go of certain memories that haunt him. Chief among these memories is the relationship he had with his father.

Many of Old Man's experiences reveal his strength of character and how well he copes with a chaotic environment. Often he acts as a "knight to the rescue," helping others in precarious situations. However, there are times when he refuses to face the reality in front of him; it is these moments that cause Old Man to face unfortunate consequences.

I decided to differentiate between Old Man's life on the street and his more secure times. During these more normal times, he is referred to as Henry, his given name. Whether Henry or Old Man, our central character cares about other people. In both identities, he possesses a moral code and struggles to do the right thing.

Old Man's journey is long and arduous. His strength of character becomes his best friend as he navigates his way around a seemingly inevitable resolution. Each surprise in his life is a chapter of a fairy tale.

Robert A. Pauker
Fairfield County, Connecticut

Acknowledgements

I want to express my sincere gratitude posthumously to my good friend, Lee Blum, who read an early version of this manuscript in 2015. Lee offered me the critical perspective of an artist, as well as the encouragement of someone who cared about me.

I also want to thank Diane de Cristo who has helped me through the years to publish both personal and professional books. Diane's great advice and insights have been invaluable. Without her expertise, I would be at a loss.

I have been blessed to benefit from the analytical skills of my significant other, Barbara Edelheit. Her commentaries and logic have pushed me to have a better understanding of my plot and my characters.

Finally, I want to thank my sons, Andrew and Benjamin, and my daughters-in-law, Jill and Ali, for their constant upbeat faith in me.

· 1 ·

Jack Daniels and Creamed Spinach

Henry knew he was going to be in trouble. But he couldn't help himself. He was obsessed with the irrational, yet rational, need to have another. He looked at the empty glass next his plate of creamed spinach and filet mignon. His three favorites were right in front of him. That is, almost. His glass of Jack Daniels was empty. Even the ice cubes had been chewed.

Henry was aware of the time. The clock was getting closer and closer to the time of his presentation. He had been preparing for this presentation since the end of August; it was now the first week of October. He had begged Mr. Ciecle to give him this job. Now, he regretted it. *I should be going over everything*, Henry thought. But the temptation of another Jack Daniels to wash down the final bites of creamed spinach and steak was just too much. Since college, nearly twenty years ago, Jack Daniels had been his drink of choice. Now, it offered him a comfort from stress.

Henry's team leader had made it clear that this presentation was top priority. If those listening bought his ideas, Henry's consulting firm would reap hundreds of thousands of dollars, and Henry would earn himself the largest commission of his career. *I should be going over everything*, Henry, again, repeated to himself. For some reason Henry's self-confidence had ruptured. The lure of one more drink had won out over a celebration of many drinks later in the day. It was getting through the moment that mattered.

So, with a spontaneous gesture, Henry signaled the waiter over. "I'll have another," he said pointing to the empty glass next to his plate. *I wonder if I am slurring a word or two,* Henry thought. The waiter seemed to look at him a little funny as he requested his third Jack Daniels.

Liquor had been Henry's companion and nemesis since high school. It started with typical high school parties where Henry learned that vodka was the safe drink because his breath did not wreak of liquor. He watched his parents, who only drank Scotch, mark the liquor bottles with a microscopic dot. Since his parents never drank vodka, Henry found it easy to transfer the clear vodka to a water bottle he kept in his room and refill the vodka bottle with cold tap water to the mark made by the microscopic dot. He would take a small sip of vodka from the water bottle two or three times a week. After a couple of months of visits to the liquor cabinet, his supply was gone. There was only water in his parents' vodka bottle.

Henry realized that to keep drinking, he would have to find a source. He didn't have to look very far. His best friend's brother was of legal age to purchase liquor. "It will cost you five dollars for me," said the brother. So, Henry dipped into his allowance and his drinking career accelerated to new heights. He hid his purchased liquor in his closet.

One day, Henry's parents had a small dinner party. One of the guests asked for a shot of vodka. "This is water," proclaimed the guest, wondering if the parents were trying to pull a fast one over on him. Henry's parents were beyond embarrassed. They were mortified. To avoid further embarrassment, his father ran to the liquor store about a block away and bought the most expensive vodka on the shelf.

Henry's parents never suspected that their son had "switched the vodka with water." They immediately blamed the cleaning lady. When Henry's mother told her son what the cleaning lady had done, Henry said nothing. Of course the cleaning lady was fired and did not receive her holiday bonus. Henry debated whether to fess up, but he never came close to confessing. Occasionally, he would feel pangs of guilt, but mum was the word.

It wasn't until college that Henry switched to Jack Daniels. His college freshman roommate's drinking habits made Henry's look amateurish. The roommate would not think of starting the day without a couple of shots of Jack Daniels. To Henry's benefit, and detriment, his roommate was very generous and was willing to share his ample supply of Jack. The two college freshmen stayed roommates through sophomore year. When the roommate transferred to another college, Henry got a job in order to supply his ingrained habit.

Henry took a couple of sips from the new glass of Jack Daniels. He moved the tumbler back and forth watching the liquor dance and sway from one side of the glass to the other. Then, he looked at his watch. The time was 1:45; he had fifteen minutes to get to his presentation. He quickly downed the rest of the drink and asked for the check. He arrived at the conference room two minutes before the presentation was scheduled to begin. The eight corporate executives and board members watched him intently as he entered the room. Henry was immediately self-conscious because he had not checked his appearance at all. He couldn't tell if he looked professional or a wreck.

As Henry tried to pull himself together, he could tell that his audience looked at him strangely. A few chuckled; one or two looked a little sick. Henry had tried to look normal, if not authoritative, when he entered. He kept hearing Ciecle's voice in the back of his mind. "When you enter a meeting, look like you are in charge." Then his mind echoed Ciecle's cardinal rules: "Be prepared. Be focused. Be at your professional best." Henry's fractured state of mind told him that his boss would be horrified.

He could see discomfort on the audience's faces. This reaction went on during his presentation. It seemed that no one was really listening to Henry's words. After a short while the facial expressions of his audience annoyed him for two reasons. First, the content of the report would determine whether or not the company should agree to a merger with a current competitor. Second, Henry had never experienced this before; usually, everyone hung on each word.

When the meeting was over, Henry courteously shook hands, then stopped in the executive bathroom. While washing his hands, he happened to gaze in the mirror. To his horror, he saw that the gaps between each of his front upper and lower teeth were filled with remnants of his lunch. Small globs of creamed spinach hung from his gums. His head throbbed.

Henry was mortified. Why hadn't he checked his teeth before the meeting? He knew this could happen. It had happened before, though not to this degree and never in front of clients.

Initially, he tried to clean the globs of spinach from between his teeth with a fingernail that was slightly longer than the others. This tactic did not work very well. Then, Henry reached into his computer case and tore a tactical triangle from a piece of paper. He did not bother to check if the piece of paper was important. At that moment, he did not care.

He quickly folded the paper into a makeshift toothpick and began the surgical process of removing the debris. Fortunately, no one from the company came into the men's room. At the back of his mind was the thought that everyone knew he was in there.

Finally, the last vestige of creamed spinach was removed. Then, Henry's anxiety returned. "Should I apologize?" He thought to himself. "Should I say anything? Or, should I just leave?"

He took a deep breath, walked out of the bathroom, down the hall and out of the corporate suite. He hoped not to be noticed.

This ended his consumption of creamed spinach and filet mignon but not his love of the foods. The idea of eating at an expensive restaurant was now unthinkable. His longing for Jack Daniels was harder to suppress; however, once he was relegated to living in the streets, Henry pushed his desire downward. At times it was as if he were fighting against gravity, but his resistance prevailed. Perhaps it was partially out of the guilt he carried with him from that fateful day's presentation and partially because of poverty.

Now, all these years later, he craved for what inevitably brought back a bad memory. On most days, his yearning for his favorite meal would have been a moot point. He no longer had an expense account; he no longer had a good paycheck; in fact, he no longer had any paycheck. He was one year too young for social security, even though he looked old enough to have received a monthly government check for more than a decade or two. He had no real source of income. His parents had died broke as a result of terrible business decisions, and he had not seen his brother since leaving rehab nearly two decades ago. He had sworn to himself that his drinking days were over, but on this day something clicked inside of him. He couldn't stop thinking of the culinary triumvirate that did him in.

Sixty-one was not really old at all. But deep inside, Old Man felt that he was one hundred. *I feel like a very old man*, he would tell himself over and over. It was this thought that resulted in Henry's new name. *I will just call myself Old Man from this day on*, he concluded.

But on this day when he desperately wanted to once again experience creamed spinach, filet mignon and, of course, Jack Daniels, a miracle happened. Actually, two miracles. The first miracle happened an hour before; Old Man found a twenty-dollar bill lodged between a stone bench and a planter filled with dying mums. The second miracle happened because of the first one. Feeling lucky for the first time in multiple months, he stopped at a nearby newspaper store and bought five, two-dollar scratch-off lottery tickets. He put the remaining ten dollars in his pocket.

I don't have a coin to scratch off the tickets, he thought. Then, he looked down and saw a penny lying on the ground just a few inches from where he stood. He didn't wait to see if anyone was walking by; he just reached and grabbed the penny.

For the first time in a long time, Old Man prayed. "Please, God." He repeated these words over and over. He returned to the bench next to the community flowerpot where he sat down to see his lottery fate.

The first two tickets – nothing. Maybe his luck had run out. But on the third scratch lottery ticket he won $5.00. His spirits lifted. He slowly scratched the surface from the fourth ticket.

He decided to scratch the entire covering off and then look. He gazed at each number; his eyes stopped at the second number of the bottom row. He looked at this number twice and, then three times. He started to smile, revealing his spinach-free teeth that had deteriorated significantly over the past two decades. "$100.00," he mumbled to himself over and over.

He took the ticket, forgetting that he had one unscratched instant left, and walked as fast as he could to the newspaper shop. "I won," he shouted. His voice was much raspier than it had been years before. "I won."

The clerk willingly gave Old Man $105. In the back of his mind had been the fear that the clerk would refuse to give him his money on some kind of technicality. Between the bench and the newspaper store, he had imagined the clerk saying, "Sorry, you are wrong." Or, "Sorry, you didn't scratch the ticket right. It doesn't count."

But none of that happened. The clerk gave him his money. "Thank you, thank you," Old Man shouted.

Now, he wanted to celebrate. All he could think about was Jack Daniels, filet mignon and creamed spinach. His mind quickly cut back to the moment he left rehab about twenty years ago. He hadn't had a drink since the day he sipped Jack Daniels from a paper cup next to the fountain. *That was a long time ago. I have been good,* he thought. But the pull to celebrate was like a gravitational force dragging him down. He stopped in his tracks, closed his eyes, and took a deep breath. He thought about his many years living in the street. *I deserve a reward*, he concluded.

Old Man wasn't sure where to go. It had been a long time since he had been to a restaurant. *Will they let me in? I look like a homeless person*. Then, he laughed at himself. *I am a homeless person—sort of.*

He wandered down the central part of the city, keeping his left hand in his pocket to make sure that his money remained safe. Periodically, he would fondle the two fifty-dollar bills that the clerk had given him to make sure they were real.

I have to clean up. I can't look like this. I can't smell. His internal monologue continued. *Maybe I can buy a new shirt. I haven't bought a new shirt for a long time. Where can I buy a shirt? How much will it cost? This money needs to last. Maybe it would have been easier not to win anything. Then, I wouldn't have to figure anything out.*

Old Man continued to wander through the central part of the city where the outdoor shopping mall prohibited automobiles. The foot traffic was light. He looked in store windows. One store window showed three manikins wearing men's shirts. He stopped to look. He shouted out loud, "Thirty five dollars!" He kept wandering.

By chance, he took a right turn down a narrow street where he had never been. About halfway down the street, he saw a store sign that read: Used Clothing. At first, he hesitated. *Maybe they will throw me out*, he thought. But he went in anyway.

The clerk was cautiously helpful and Old Man left with a white long sleeve shirt that he purchased for $6. He didn't try it on because he worried that his body odor would contaminate the shirt. *I hope it fits*, he thought. *Now where to clean up?*

The last time Old Man had showered was about three weeks ago at a local shelter. He had managed to spray wash himself in the fountain at the center of the pedestrian mall a few times.

He periodically would take a quick wash in the bathroom at a local coffee house; the bathroom was located outside adjacent to the coffee house; this way, he did not have to face ridicule by going inside. On this particularly lucky day, he hoped there was soap in the dispenser at the bathroom next to the coffeehouse.

Before going to the coffee house for his sink bath, he had one stop. He hid his belongings next to a basement apartment near the center of town. He found this spot by accident years ago when running from Hungry Harry–the meanest homeless person around.

The people on the street called him Hungry Harry because he would steal food right out of your hands. He had an insatiable appetite. One time a teenager had given Old Man a ham and cheese sandwich on French bread. Just when he was ready to take a bite of the French bread, Hungry Harry snuck up from behind and grabbed the entire sandwich from his hands. Old Man let out an angry yell, but he knew better than to give chase to the likes of Harry who needed no excuse to demonstrate his personal delight in practicing violence.

One particular day a few years ago, Harry had seen an elderly woman passing by who gave Old Man a five-dollar bill. In Hungry Harry's mind that five dollars should have been his. So, he chased Old Man down the street, behind a set of stores into an alleyway. Old Man knew that Hungry Harry would seize the five dollars and accompany his act with a set of punches to the face. "Don't take what belongs to me," Harry would tell his victim between whacks.

As Old Man ran, he noticed an apartment building surrounded by a tall, green hedge. With a little effort he slipped through a slight break in the hedge just before Hungry Harry came into sight. As he ran to the apartment building, Old Man found the perfect hiding place. Next to a first-floor apartment was a rectangular stone well a few feet below the apartment window.

Old Man crouched inside the well so that he was not visible to any passersby. He could hear Harry yell, "Just give me the money and I won't hurt you." Old Man had no intention of surrendering the money. So he pushed his body as low as it would go inside the stone well, and he became invisible to the neighborhood.

That is where Old Man hid on that day in November several years ago. The stone well is where he had hid his belongings since the day after the encounter with Hungry Harry who, shortly after the chase, collapsed and died from a heart attack.

Old Man lifted the white tarp that he had gotten from a dumpster next to the stone well. He looked through the large duffle bag below the tarp that he had gotten from another dumpster. At the bottom of the bag was a pair of underwear and a pair of blue wash-and-wear pants. The underwear was relatively fresh—as he had only worn it three times after washing it in the mall fountain late at night when no one was looking. The pants had never been worn. He found them in a bag on the ground two years earlier; someone must have bought them and dropped the bag on the ground. Old Man had checked the size of the pants and it seemed close enough to his size; so, he took the bag. *It's not like stealing.* He thought back then. *If I don't take the pants, someone else will.*

With his new shirt, new pair of pants, and three-times worn underwear, Old Man walked with purpose to the bathroom next to the coffee house. He was in luck; the bathroom was empty. With some maneuvering, he spread soap from the dispenser on both hands, added water, and began to give

10

himself a type of sponge bath. Rinsing was a problem as it was difficult to get enough water from the faucet to various parts of his body. In the end, his body was as clean as it had been since the day after his shower three weeks ago. He replaced his used, smelly shirt with the new one and his old sweatpants with the blue wash and wear.

As he glanced one more time in the mirror, he thought, *What has become of me?*

He made sure that the two fifty-dollar bills and the five-dollar bill moved from one pocket to the other. He put his ragged tennis shoes and old socks back on, as there was no other option. He put his old clothes in the bag that had contained the blue pants. He tightly tied the plastic handles on the bag, sealing the noticeable odor of the clothes inside. He exited the bathroom to find two people waiting until he finished his ritual. Old Man put his head down so as not to make eye contact with the person closer to the sink.

He walked back to his hiding place to deposit the used, smelly clothes.

Finally, he was ready for Jack Daniels.

Old Man moved with a purpose along the pedestrian mall walkway. The Angus Steakhouse was about five blocks from his storage locker in the window well next to the basement apartment. The idea of ordering a Jack Daniels again in a restaurant excited him. It had been so many years. He knew that the Angus served filet mignon and creamed spinach because about six months ago he had stopped to read its menu posted in the window. He had imagined what it might be like to, again, dine inside of a good restaurant. He remembered some of his celebrated meals and shuddered when his memory perseverated on the fateful lunch that resulted in his fateful embarrassment.

As he approached the block on which the steakhouse was located, Old Man hesitated. *What if everyone stares?* He thought. *I haven't shaved in three weeks. I must look strange. What if they ask me to leave?*

His concerns caused his gait to slow down until he stopped. He was only about ten yards from the restaurant entrance. For several minutes, Old Man just stood there, relatively motionless. He did not seem to be in anyone's way. No one asked him to move. It almost seemed like he was invisible.

During the past several years, Old Man had learned to put up with almost every emotion. He learned to use his heart as a barometer of feelings. When his heart raced, he knew he must be cautious. When his heart slowed down, he knew he was in control. At this moment his heart was racing; his head pounded with a defeatist mantra that shrieked: *You don't belong here anymore!*

Then, an elderly woman, perhaps it was the same woman who had given him the five dollars years before, smiled at him. His reflexes made him return the smile. This connection gave Old Man a boost of confidence.

He tried to clear his mind. At first, he was not successful. His mind imagined what the others in the restaurant would think of someone like him sitting next to them. *Don't think of the past*, he kept telling himself. *Don't make things up*, he added. On most days, Old Man would have given up on the idea of the restaurant. But something deep inside of him left him determined to live out his fantasy. Perhaps he really wanted to relegate himself to ridicule. Or, perhaps he wanted to see if he could grasp on to any part of his past life. Regardless, he decided to keep going. So, one inhale and one exhale later he approached the front door of the Angus Steakhouse.

Memories filled his mind. How many times had he been in a similar environment? Probably hundreds—just not in the past two decades. The smells of Caesar salad, steak, and liquor rekindled a new set of memories. It was almost like he was a dog, being able to extract each individual smell from various parts of the dining room. For the first time in so, so long, he felt like he was home. At the same time, he felt like he was a stranger in a familiar land. He thought he belonged but seemed to have lost his passport.

The maître d' asked him, "May I help you?"

Old Man did not respond initially. He heard the maître d', but it was as if he was paralyzed. Then, he replied in a rather uncertain voice. "Yes. Can I sit down?"

The maître d' looked carefully at his new patron who looked quite a bit more ragged and disheveled from his typical client. However, with nothing other than a slightly quizzical look, he led Old Man to a small table between two other small tables. These tables on each side were empty.

Old Man became self-conscious when he looked to his left and saw a youngish-looking couple sitting two tables down from him. He thought, *What if I smell?* To his right, there was no one.

He became uncomfortable and was about to abandon his plan. *I don't fit in anymore*, he thought.

Just when he was about to get up to leave, a waiter came over and said, "Will you have a drink, sir?" Old Man, at first, was shocked by the question and the politeness of the question. He sat up straight in his chair. He glanced at the couple next to him who seemed to pay no attention. Then, he glanced up at the waiter. "I'll have a Jack Daniels."

"Do you want that on the rocks?"

"Yes, of course, on the rocks."

The decision to stay had been decided for him by the waiter. So, Old Man sat there waiting for his Jack Daniels, thinking about a different world filled with money, love, and hope.

· 2 ·

The Snowman

He felt guilty, at first. He could have saved the forty dollars spent on lunch. The experience gnawed at him. It was as if he were again the rich, upcoming thirty-something who had received an overwhelming inner delight from snorting cocaine, only to be let down when reality hit. For a few moments, he felt like Henry again. Then, once reality set in Old Man felt like a fool. He had sucked himself into a time vacuum that presented an instant of false hope. His reasoning floundered. Now he had to face what he really had become-- again.

The comparison grew overwhelming. Pretending to be what he used to be proved instantly gratifying. By his third Jack Daniels and second side dish of creamed spinach, it was as if he were again celebrating a multimillion-dollar deal. Once Old Man exited the restaurant's revolving door, he was back into the real world. A sudden blast of cold air made this transition even worse.

Every inch of him felt cold as he made his way back to the window well where his treasures were hidden. He was struck and almost amused that being in the restaurant had seemed so right. The Jack Daniels tasted terrific. The creamed spinach was excellent. The steak was perfect. The restaurant had done its part. Nevertheless, he was empty inside.

He walked through the outdoor mall where he had spent countless hours sitting, waiting, and asking for a handout. He no longer imagined. He just shivered. He had not expected it to start snowing. There were one or two inches of snow on the ground. The snow must have begun just after he arrived at the restaurant.

As Old Man moved to the edge of the fountain in the center of the mall, his body suddenly felt a giant, unfriendly push. It was as if he were smacked intentionally. Without hesitation, he lurched forward. He could sense that the creamed spinach was backing up in his system.

Instinctively, Old Man looked up to see a muscular, thirtyish man, wearing an expensive Burberry coat, whisk by his right shoulder. The young man seemed to have a smirk on his face; he said nothing as he walked by.

Old Man's surprise became rage. He was sure the man in the Burberry coat had pushed him intentionally. His back experienced a sudden surge of tightness and discomfort. For an instant, it remained numb. Then, Old Man shocked himself; he had not felt this much anger in years. Since he had become a man of the streets, he had learned to put up with a lot. It was not uncommon for him to be mocked or ridiculed; no matter how vicious the comments, he did not respond. However, this was a physical assault. The other physical assaults were by other people of the street. This one was by someone who was just like he used to be.

Old Man quickened his pace. With a deliberate walk, he caught up with the bully in a matter of two-dozen steps. He tapped the bully on his shoulder. The young man turned around while slowing his pace.

In a loud voice Old Man said, "Why did you push me?"

The bully only smiled. With a deliberate gesture, he raised the larger middle finger of his right hand far enough in the air so that Old Man could see the movement but not too high, trying to shield his response from others passing by.

Old Man became further incensed. He searched desperately for the right thing to say. Finally, he blurted out in the loudest voice he could muster. "Didn't your mother teach you any manners?"

The bully was taken aback by the nature of his combatant's response. "You don't count," said the young man. "I saw you in the restaurant. Scum like you shouldn't be allowed in."

Old Man stared at the bully for a moment. He wanted to say something but any successful response escaped him. He wanted to use his strong left arm in retaliation. But, he backed off. So, he looked at the young man again and raised his larger middle finger on his left hand as a parting gesture.

This encounter lasted less than a minute but it left Old Man exhausted.

Even though he was cold, he decided to sit on the edge of the fountain in the center of the outdoor mall to catch his breath. He watched the snow. He thought of the bully and, then he thought of nothing. Initially the incident had left him feeling drained and, then, ashamed. For a second he blamed himself for not being quick enough to respond to the bully's indictment. However, after his immediate internal struggle, he managed to bury his shame deep inside.

Within a moment or two, Old Man spontaneously stuck out his tongue, as he had done when a child and let an occasional snowflake land. He mused. For a minute, he was happy. He thought of his father. He thought of his unhappy childhood, except for that special moment. He flinched when visualizing his father staring at him on the edge of the fountain. He imagined his father asking, "How could this happen to my son?"

With his hands, Old Man began playing with the snow, picking up small amounts and squeezing the flakes into his bare hands. The vision of the special moment with his father had numbed him to the extreme cold of the snow. Old Man sighed. *For a minute of happiness, I feel an eternity of unhappiness.*

Then, almost arbitrarily, he began to mold the snow into a ball about the size of a volleyball. He placed the ball of snow on the ledge of the fountain next to him. More purposefully, Old Man created a second ball of snow slightly smaller than the first one. He magnetically placed this second ball on top of the first. His hands now made a third ball of snow and he placed this one on the top. *A snowman*, he thought. "A miniature snowman," he said aloud.

Old Man was suddenly amused. *I haven't made a snowman since I was a child.*

"Look, that man is making a snowman," shouted a little boy to his mother. The boy ran to the edge of fountain where the snowman rested on the ledge that surrounded the fountain.

Old Man smiled. "His hands must be cold," said the little boy. His mother looked at him. "Mommy, can I give him my gloves?" At first, the boy's mother remained silent and expressionless. After a brief reflection, the mother nodded.

"Here," the boy said to Old Man. "You need these."

Old Man at first refused the boy's kindness. Then, he merely smiled and said, "Thank you."

It didn't matter if the gloves fit. Old Man felt his eyes filling with tears. Kindness. That was something usually foreign to him.

The boy asked, "Aren't you going to finish it?" Old Man looked at the boy and nodded.

Surprisingly, Old Man could squeeze the gloves onto his hands, albeit they were quite tight. Their warmth helped to thaw his fingers a little bit. He thought of the boy's kindness. His mind traveled to an era of the past. For a long instant Old Man thought of life years ago, well before this moment of steakhouses. He briefly pretended that his imaginary child, a daughter, was there next to the wall of the fountain. He wondered how his life could have been different if only he and Ginny had a family. His moment of reflection haunted his mind. He mumbled a few words to himself that sounded like, "I am so lonely. God forgive me for wasting my life." Then, he silently sang the first line of his favorite song.

You are the sunshine of my life

Suddenly, Old Man remembered that the boy was still there in front of him. "The snowman needs some eyes," he told the boy. "What should we use?"

The boy thought for a second. Then, he reached into his pocket and pulled out two pennies. "Here," the boy said, handing the pennies to him.

"Good idea," said Old Man who first looked at the boy's mother to make sure it was all right to use the pennies. The mother nodded slightly. He asked the boy, "How's this?" Then, he placed the pennies near the top of the smallest ball of snow. The pennies were too big for the face, but it didn't matter to the boy.

"That looks good," the boy answered. "But now you need a nose."

"A nose. A nose," repeated Old Man. He looked lost. Just at the moment the little boy brought up the idea of a nose, an elderly lady was walking by. The lady noticed the small crowd around the snowman. She heard the boy's comments.

The lady stopped near the two of them; she reached into her shopping bag. "Here," she said, handing Old Man a small carrot that she had pulled out of a bag.

"Wow," said the little boy. "That is cool."

Old Man pushed the large end of the carrot into the snow just below and in between the two pennies. It took a few tries to get the carrot to stay in place.

"Now he has to have a mouth," stated the little boy.

The boy's mother reached for her son's hand and whispered, "We have to go." The boy protested but the mother was firm. "We can stop back after we go to the doctor," the mother reassured the boy.

Old Man heard the mother's comment and, secretly hoped that the boy was not seriously ill. He thought about asking the mother but immediately decided to say nothing. So, the boy, who had been a source of inspiration, and the mother, who had been tolerant, left.

After taking a few steps, the boy shouted back at Old Man. "What is your name.?"

"My name is Old Man."

"You don't look that old," answered the boy.

Old Man sat for a moment. A tear came to his eye. He felt the boy's kindness and his heart experienced a rare feeling of warmth.

Then, he looked up.

"Use this for the mouth," a young man who appeared to be in his late teens said. It was a piece of red licorice.

So Old Man broke the licorice in half and then shoved one piece into the snowman's face until it appeared to be smiling. The redness of the smile was quite a contrast to the copper of the pennies and the orange of the carrot.

By now, the snowman was attracting a small crowd. "It needs a hat," yelled a passerby. Old Man waved.

"Here, I have another one at home," said a little girl who handed Old Man her stocking cap. He motioned for the little girl to put her cap on the snowman's head. She looked at her mother who nodded.

"There," the little girl said as she placed the cap on top of the third ball of snow. Old Man laughed.

He stared at the snowman. Something was missing. Finally, he realized that the arms were missing. He reached over across the walkway and grabbed two sticks next to a nearby tree that had escaped the town clean up. He placed the sticks on the left and right sides of the middle snowball. He was done.

A few people had remained to watch the completion. They applauded. One middle-aged woman took a dollar bill from her pocket and gave it to him. He was instantly confused. *I am wearing the best clothes I have*, he thought. *How can they tell?*

A few seconds later, another person handed Old Man another dollar. This was followed by a third, fourth, and fifth contribution. He sat there, letting the dollars rest next to him. He felt both grateful and embarrassed. He had just spent about forty dollars on lunch and now strangers were giving him money when he did not ask for it.

He thought about all of the days he had spent asking for money. He thought about the numbers of people who would walk right by him. He thought about the scores of people who would scoff at how he looked. On these days, he begged for money and usually received little. At this moment, he did not ask for help but received a week or two's worth of begging. *Ironic*, Old Man thought, *how ironic!*

He sat next to the snowman for a while. Occasionally, he looked at his pile of dollars that now totaled forty-four. Soon, the mall was nearly empty. He was more or less alone with the snowman that had become hardened by the increasingly colder temperatures. He had forgotten about the cold. Now, he began to shiver.

Finally, Old Man got up. He saluted his creation. He, again, walked towards the well next to the window where his treasures were hidden.

On his way, he saw an old woman who looked much older than he. She was sitting along the side of the outdoor mall, in the snow, at the corner next to a high-end clothing store. Old Man noticed the woman from several feet away. Her face was covered with an old plaid scarf; her feet were shaking. He did not recognize her.

He approached the woman, even though he sensed her fright. He was often like she was—cold and alone.

Why was he bothering her? Her body started to recoil. She looked at him but said nothing. She was getting ready to attack. What did he want? She had almost nothing.

Old Man got closer to the old woman. With each step, she recoiled tighter and tighter. Finally, he was next to her. She wanted to scream but could not. So she just stared. He reached into his pocket and pulled out the forty or so dollar bills he had been given. He estimated one-half the pile and put the money in his left and right hands.

He asked, "Which do you want?" "This one," holding up his left hand "or this one," holding up his right hand. The old woman did not move. "Which one?" His voice became authoritarian. The old woman pointed to his left hand. "Here," he yelled and dropped half of the money into her lap.

The old woman grabbed the money. She immediately counted it, still in disbelief. She thought it was a trick. Only after Old Man slowly walked away did the woman put the money inside of her shirt.

Old Man skipped as he went back to his treasures. At first, he felt a lift from his act of charity; then, his mind turned to what he had become.

· 3 ·

Another Act of Kindness

He couldn't get the old woman's image out of his mind. She was beyond repair. Her destiny was locked. "Unlike Miriam," he mumbled. He could hear Miriam's voice.

"Sometimes I feel like I am trapped—trapped by people who don't really care. They have taken my money and now look at me. At times I pray to God to give me strength to make it. At other times, I curse a God who has left me so alone. All I really want is peace."

Old Man remembered how he held Miriam. He only found out her name just before she left him. He tried to sooth her anguish. He spoke of sunny days and warm winds. He spoke of giving and sharing. "I will get us an ice cream. Do you like ice cream?" She nodded. "I will be back."

She begged, "Don't leave. Don't go anywhere. OK?"

Old Man knew if he did not return soon, Miriam would be gone. She was distraught. Distraught people do spontaneous things. They were not predictable. This chapter of his life had been filled with distraught people—people who had run out of options; people who had lost one kind of freedom to gain another.

Old Man had seen Miriam resting against a cement wall in the alleyway behind Fein's Hardware. It was obvious that she had been crying. She was emotionally frazzled. He sat down next to her. He asked, "Why are you like this?"

He had never seen her before. She seemed out of place. She did not push him away. It appeared that she was grateful for someone to notice. She looked at him. "I am alone."

"We are all alone here," he answered. "What happened to you?"

"My daughter yelled at me. She told me I was a problem. She told me I was a burden." Old Man listened as Miriam talked about how she had moved in with her daughter a few months ago. She had given up her apartment. She thought life would be wonderful. She would be with her granddaughter. Her daughter was in money trouble. "I was happy to give her what I had."

"For a little while everything was ok," she continued. "Then, my daughter started yelling at me for anything. She told me I was pressuring her. She told me I was too neat when I picked up. She told me not to tell her how to raise my granddaughter."

"It didn't take long for things to become unbearable." Miriam cried for a moment. "What kind of a monster had I raised?"

She looked at Old Man and shook her head. "Yesterday, she screamed at me for stealing twenty dollars from her purse. Twenty dollars! I have been paying half of the mortgage and paying for my granddaughter's lunches. Now I am a thief?"

"My daughter told me that I was making her life miserable. I left. I just left. I walked to the bus stop. I kept looking over my shoulder waiting for her to come after me. She didn't. I arrived at the bus stop. When the bus came, I took it to town. I left the house with the five dollars I had in my coat pocket. Nothing else."

"I need to hurry," Old Man mumbled as he tried to figure out how to get her an ice cream. He had no money, but he had made a promise. In his heart he knew that Miriam might do something drastic unless she could have one good experience that might change her look on life. *I have to find a few dollars to get back with an ice cream. I have to make this happen*, he thought.

So he walked to the corners of Main and Dime Streets. He began to beg. "I have a sick friend. Can you spare a little change?" Of course no one believed him. One passerby did drop a quarter in his hand, being careful not touch an old man's cooties.

After several minutes, he was desperate. He walked the extra block to the fountain. He noticed a young woman talking on her cell phone. Next to her was her purse that was wide open resting on the cement wall that surrounded the fountain. He knew what he was thinking contradicted every ounce of morality that was left inside of him. He knew he should walk away.

Old Man approached the fountain. He sat on the stone wall in front of the fountain next to the girl's purse. She paid no attention. He looked around. No one seemed to care that he was next to the purse. He stopped thinking. He rationalized right and wrong. He would do one wrong for a bigger right.

He stopped rationalizing and reached into the purse. No one seemed to notice. His hand groped for what seemed like a wallet. The girl paid no attention. She continued her animated conversation. The people approaching him appeared oblivious. Old Man grabbed what he was sure was a wallet. He put the wallet under his leg. He sat there quietly with a sweat pouring down his brow. He continued to look around. He heard the girl say, "OK, I have another stop to make and then I will be home." He knew she was finished. Spontaneously, he slipped the wallet into his coat pocket. It was the large right pocket—big enough for a pint of Jack Daniels. He looked the other way and got up from the stonewall. The girl was just getting ready to put her phone in her purse.

He walked away. When he was about half a football field on the other side of the fountain, he turned around. He expected either the girl or the police to be there. He did not feel anyone's breath. In the distance, he saw the girl getting up from the fountain wall. Her purse was still open. She moved away as if nothing was wrong.

Old Man circled around the fountain and walked back towards a dark alley on the other side of the fountain. He ducked into an apartment building entrance where he grabbed the wallet from his right pocket and opened it. He found $60 in small bills. He grabbed two five-dollar bills and put the wallet back in his right pocket. That should be more than enough, he thought. He walked towards the ice cream shop.

He bought a large ice cream sundae, covered with fudge and whip cream. He asked for two cherries on top. For himself, he got a simple vanilla ice cream cone—one scoop. He walked as quickly as he could towards the alleyway wall where he had first seen Miriam. In his heart he did not expect her to be there. When he turned the final corner, he saw her sitting on the ground leaning against the wall motionless. His heart now sank. He got closer. Old Man's spirits rose as he heard the welcome guttural sounds of the woman snoring. "Get up," he said quietly. "I have your ice cream. I know it's cold outside but this will make you feel better."

"You really came back," she said. "I didn't think you would."

Old Man smiled. He handed her the ice cream sundae that had just melted a little bit. "I haven't had one of these since I was a little girl." She paused. "That was a long time ago."

Old Man stayed with the woman until she finished. He ate his ice cream cone slowly to make sure he did not finish ahead of her. "Let's go," he said.

"Go where?"

"I will take you to your daughter's house."

The woman argued. "She doesn't want any part of me."

"I will make you a bet," he said. "If we get there and she doesn't want to see you, then I promise I will take care of you." He knew his words were a risk. The last thing he needed was to take care of her. But in his heart, he felt that he said what he had to say.

The woman was clearly conflicted. In her heart, she wanted to go, but her fear created a boundary that made taking the risk so difficult. "I just can't," she responded to him but did not run away. She trusted Old Man even though she had just met him. Deep down inside she wanted to see her daughter and, especially, her granddaughter. It didn't take much to convince her about the right thing to do.

"Look around," he said. "What do you see? You see people like me who have nowhere to go. You see people who have no one to turn to. You have someone. If this daughter of yours is at all like you, she is something special. Don't lose this chance. There is no one else to get you there because you won't go there yourself." Old Man looked into her eyes. "She had a bad few days. I know your daughter loves you."

She was coming around. He held her hand. "My destiny is already set," he said. "You have another chance."

The woman thought. "How will we get there? It is fifteen miles away."

At first Old Man wasn't sure. Then, he remembered the wallet. "Just give me a second," he said and went into a doorway a few feet from where the old woman sat. He looked around to make sure that no one saw him take the remaining fifty dollars from the wallet and put the two twenties, a five, and five ones in the right pocket of his pants.

"We will take a cab," he said.

So it was. The two of them looked out of place as they haled a cab alongside of the man in a three-piece suit and the elderly lady with three shopping bags filled with just-purchased clothes. Of course, no cab stopped for them. Old Man remembered his corporate days. He recalled how easy it was to summon a cab. Now, no driver would stop. This was the case until about a half hour later when one driver stopped.

Old Man pulled the woman into the back seat of the cab. Even though he had bathed in the sink, his body now did give off a subtle fragrance of body odor. When the driver smelled the fragrance, he started to tell the two to get out. But before the driver could command the two passengers, Old Man yelled out the address and showed the driver the fifty dollars he had taken from the wallet. He asked, "Will this get us there?" The driver nodded. When the driver was halfway, Old Man added, "By the way, you have to bring me back."

"I am not going all the way back to town," replied the cab driver. "I will bring you to the edge of town where you can catch a bus."

Old Man took two dollars from the fifty for bus fare. The driver would have to make do with forty-eight dollars.

The woman began to tremble as the cab got closer to the house. She grabbed his hand. "Will you come in with me?"

He shook his head no. "I care about you. But I do not belong here. I am not unhappy where I am. You need to go there alone."

When the cab approached the house, a little girl was playing in the front yard. The front door was open. Old Man could see the woman's daughter gazing out at the cab. "Time," he said to her. "I will wait until you get to the front door. If you need to, you can run back to the cab."

She looked at him. "Miriam," she said. "My name is Miriam. That is my wonderful granddaughter. My special, beautiful granddaughter!"

Miriam opened the back door of the cab. She walked slowly down the driveway. Her daughter looked through the storm door. At first Miriam was obscured by a large oak tree at the base of the driveway. The daughter wondered who was this person coming up the driveway; her first instinct was to run out and grab her child who was still playing in the front yard oblivious to her grandmother's steps towards the house. The granddaughter did not notice her; she was intently playing with her giant stuffed panda that Miriam had given her.

When Miriam had taken half-dozen steps, she stopped and looked at her daughter who had just come through the storm door onto the front porch. Old Man watched. For an instant, he was afraid that he had pushed the woman to do something that was not good. "Maybe I was wrong," he muttered.

Then, mother and daughter ran to each other. Both were crying. The little girl began crying also. She probably didn't know why; she just wanted to fit in. Instinctively, the three began hugging each other.

Old Man told the driver to go quickly. He did not want to be there when Miriam looked back at the cab. He didn't want any temptation to join her family. His destiny was set. He did not want to impose his fate on anyone else.

When Old Man got off the bus near the fountain, he looked for a police officer. It took a few minutes but he did find one. He made sure that no one was looking. He carefully took the wallet from the pocket with his right hand. He dropped the wallet on the ground. "Officer," he yelled. "There is a wallet on the ground."

The officer bent over to pick it up. He glared for a moment at Old Man. Then, the officer relaxed. "Thank you. You are an honest man. I will make sure it gets back to whoever it belongs to," said the policeman.

· 4 ·

The Childhood Fantasy

Old Man remembered his love for flying kites. As a child, his father had taken him on that one special day to the open field at the top of the hill near their home to fly his triangular kite. This day held sacred within Old Man's memory. Never had he been happier. Never had his father shown such love and enthusiasm for his son who desperately craved every spoonful a dad could mouth.

The father showed his son how to tie the thin white string to the wooden structure of the kite. "We have to make sure the knots are small, but secure," the father said.

As the son ran along the open field with the father behind holding the kite in the air, he looked back to make sure that this wonderful moment was not a dream.

At just the right moment, with a gust of wind at hand, the father gently pushed the kite up into the air. Within an instant, the son felt the string's tightening around his wrist. Then, he looked up and squealed with delight.

The kite soared into the wind. "Let out the string," said the father. The son did as he was told with delight.

This day, this series of moments, remained cemented into Old Man's memory. He never again experienced this same feeling of love and excitement coming from his father. The day was part of his salvation—his purpose for living. Often, as he sat freezing in the snow or getting soaked by the rain, he would warm his insides by reliving this day.

Now, at this crucial juncture of his questionable life, he would experience another moment that would remind him of his beloved childhood memory.

The day was an unusually warm winter day not too long after he had given part of his financial good fortunes to the old lady and had built the snowman with the boy.

For some undeterminable reason, Old Man walked aimlessly for hours on end. Periodically, he would stop at select corners and spend a brief time begging for money. "I need to eat," he would say to passersby. He found this to be the best of his begging lines. For some reason, people seemed to respond to the word "need." He guessed it was because everyone needs to eat.

At one intersection he managed to collect just over five dollars rather quickly. He was very hungry. He wandered away from the corner wondering what to buy with his earnings. As he walked, his right eye caught a vision that reminded him of his past. In the window of a store selling "used toys" was a kite, not too unlike the kite he flew with his father. Next to the kite was a small sign that read: "classic kite, only $4.50."

Old Man stared at the kite and, of course, his mind filled with those precious, unforgettable moments with his father. An uncontrollable urge overcame him. He went into the toyshop.

"The kite," he said. "The kite. How much?"

The teenage clerk went over to the sign in the window. "The sign says $4.50."

Old Man thought for a moment. "Is there string with it?"

"I don't know to be honest," said the teenager. "I think you are going to have to buy the string somewhere else."

"I only have $5.00," Old Man said. "I have to have string to fly it."

The boy looked at Old Man sympathetically. Perhaps the teenager thought of his own grandfather or perhaps he could see that look of hopeful helplessness in the eyes of his customer. "Let me look in the back and see if I can find some string."

The clerk exited through a beaded curtain into a back room. Old Man just stood at the precise location that the teenager had left him. He knew that the boy was new to his job. The owner would never have left anyone in Old Man's category of life alone in the front of the shop.

"You are in luck. I found some string," said the clerk, holding up a rolled ball of kite string that had been used before.

Old Man nodded his approval. "I will give you the string and the kite for the $4.50."

Old Man smiled. The deal was done. He walked out of the store with fifty cents in his pocket and a kite in his hands.

He carefully embraced the kite, protecting it from small gusts of wind and from careless bystanders who might bump into its outstretched wooden frame.

His heart led him to the obvious place. The walk lasted a long time. Old Man was focused. By the time he climbed the hill, his feet were soaked from stepping into the puddles of melted snow. He did not notice.

As he climbed the hill, he thought of his father. He thought of how both of their lives had been a disappointment to so many. He thought about how that one special day with his father almost made up for how his life had turned out.

When Old Man got to the field at the top of the hill, he realized that it was no longer an empty field. It was covered with a half dozen houses. His dream of flying his kite in the same open field was gone.

At first, he wanted to give up and walk down the hill. But his instincts told him to make the best out of a bad situation. His heart told him to look for a path.

So he looked for a place to fly his kite. The obvious choice was to fly the kite on the road dividing the six large houses into two sides of three. He tied the string to the kite's frame just as his father had shown him.

The road seemed so short. He thought to himself, *How can I get enough wind?* As his mind dictated selected cautions, his arms forcefully pushed the kite into the air. His legs gained speed by the end of the second house on the left side of the road. And his eyes followed the kite upward.

"A miracle," he mumbled to himself. Because there was substantial distance between houses, Old Man had some distance to run before he came to the end of the road. Fortunately, the road was deserted.

By the end of the third house on the left, the kite was clearly aloft. He smiled. It was like a dream to him. He had not been so happy in a long time. His mind was covered with his father's smile. For an instant, the kite dancing in the air reminded him of an ice cube swirling in a glass of Jack Daniels. Old Man tried with all his might to remove this image from his mind. *I can't link the two*, he thought. *I can't ruin my one happy memory.*

As the dancing ice cube was pushed from his mind, Old Man began to run back towards the beginning of the road. The kite continued to gain height. He forgot about his real age. His feet seemed to fly.

He didn't notice the new Chrysler that pulled into the driveway of the first house at the end of the street. The car stopped. Two children and their mother got out. They were headed into their home when the younger of the children exclaimed, "Look! A kite."

The little boy and his brother ran to the end of the driveway. Their curious mother trailed. "I wonder who he is," she said. The trio stared for a few moments.

Almost immediately, another car pulled into the next driveway. Out of this Ford came a little girl and her mother. They had noticed their neighbors gathered next to the road as they turned into the driveway. "What's going on?" The little girl yelled to the younger boy.

He responded, "Look over there. A kite!"

"Look mommy." The little girl inquired, "Who is that man?"

The mother decided to find out. She told her daughter to run over to her neighbor's driveway and stay with the others.

Then, the mother walked over to Old Man whose gait had slowed as his stamina dwindled.

She yelled, "Who are you?" The mother was a little frightened as she asked the question. But her demeanor did not reveal her concern. Her voice sounded quite authoritarian. Her first inclination had been to call the police. Something, some instinct, told her to ask first.

Old Man did not notice the mother. She was coming right towards him, but his eyes were riveted on the kite.

The mother repeated her question. "Who are you?" This time he stopped and noticed her.

At first he bumbled for a response. Who was he? Even he didn't know. Implicitly he did know that a police car was one answer away. So, he replied as clearly as his raspy voice would allow. "I used to fly kites here with my father when I was a little boy." Somehow Old Man knew that this answer would not be enough.

"Well, you are going to have to leave," said the mother.

Old Man felt the string on his kite grow less rigid and could feel the kite falling. He looked up just in time to catch the kite before it smashed on the ground. "I will leave," he said. "Please let me wind the string and then I will go."

At that moment a third car entered the street. This one stopped near Old Man and the mother. The passenger in the back seat of the car rolled down his window. Old Man heard a voice that was vaguely familiar. "Look, Mommy, it is the guy who made the snowman in town."

Old Man stared at the boy and remembered. He remembered the boy offering his gloves, and he remembered the boy's concern. He remembered the mother and how she encouraged her son.

The boy asked, "Do you remember me?" Old Man nodded. "Were you flying that kite?" Old Man nodded. "Wow, I would like to see that."

The two mothers looked at each other. The mother of the little girl stated loudly that she did not like the idea of a street person staying around the neighborhood. The mother who Old Man had seen at the fountain seemed to be sympathetic.

Old Man was dead in his tracks. He picked up the kite that had fallen to the ground. He was bewildered. *Do I stay or do I go? Am I welcome or am I a pariah?* His heart beat rapidly as he wrestled with these questions.

He did not want trouble. He just wanted to feel free once more. He wanted to see his one happy childhood memory appear on the surface of the kite.

The two mothers continued to look at each other. Old Man knew he had to go. He quickly wound up his kite string into a ball and lifted the kite to his side. He began to walk down the hill away from the houses. Suddenly, he heard the familiar voice of the little boy.

"Fly it. Fly it."

Old Man smiled. He used his remaining energy to fling the kite up into the air. He began running down the hill away from the houses. "Please don't let me fall," he begged. His feet gained speed and the kite remained in the air. The little boy cheered.

"Wow," he exclaimed.

Old Man ran as far as he could before slowing down. Then, he was exhausted. Immediately, the kite fell to the ground. His heart raced. His smile was so grand that every one of his hundreds of wrinkles showed. For a few moments, he was at peace.

He looked back at the boy on the top of the hill and yelled, "Do you want the kite?"

The boy smiled and yelled back, "You keep it for next time."

Old Man carried his kite and string to his treasure trough next to the apartment building. His heart remained excited. He imagined the kite flying as he ran down the large hill and the little boy yelling, "Wow!" over and over again.

He had not had such a good day in a very long time.

His kite barely fit into the storage area. I have to be careful. Spring is not too far away. *I will want to take this out in the spring*, he thought to himself.

As he left the old building where he stored his belongings, he wondered what to do next. Most days he was happy just to sit somewhere and do nothing. Once in a while he found a book to read on the ground or in the garbage. When this happened, he would spend his afternoon reading. He was not particular about the topic. He just would be excited to learn. One day he found a book about knitting. Old Man had no yarn; he just pretended to practice the stitches. As people passed by, he would hear comments such as, "That old man should be locked up."

Some days, Old Man did not have the patience to learn. On these days he would not be content to sit on a bench and read. He would spend a good part of his day walking. Being on the street did give him a lot of exercise.

· 5 ·

The Scam

He was never lazy. In his new life every day's survival was like a job. In a sense he was his own company president. When he had worked in the traditional sense, it was easier. He was told what to do, and he received a paycheck. He knew where to go for food. He had a place to go for shelter. Now there was nothing taken for granted. Every decision made a difference. Deep down inside, Old Man saw survival as a challenge. He actually thrived by living on the edge. This wasn't true for everyone. But there was a select group.

He did actual work one time following the exit through the revolving door. It happened a few months after he ran out of money and had to leave his one room basement apartment. When he lived in his other corporate world, Henry had volunteered twice a month at the homeless shelter on Kane Street. He helped out in the kitchen, preparing meals and cleaning up. The woman who ran the kitchen was extremely possessive of her domain. As a result, she was not the most pleasant person to be around. But she could cook!

The lines for the noon meal would be around the block. Anyone could eat. In order to get the dinner meal, you had to be selected by the daily lottery to stay overnight in the shelter. Sometimes a hundred men needing a place to stay would line up between four and four-thirty. Each would receive a number. At 4:31, the shelter director would spin a cage filled with numbers. If your number was called, you had a place for the night, a free dinner and a hot shower. If your number was not called, you were given a sandwich, usually American cheese, and wished good luck.

Henry left his final apartment with a large suitcase filled with stuff—some of which was non-essential for daily survival. The original suitcase even contained a small hair dryer and other possessions that offered no real daily assistance. He learned. It wasn't long before the weight of the suitcase went from forty pounds to twenty-five. However, Henry kept the hair dryer. *You never know*, he thought.

During these first few months on his own, Henry gravitated towards what he knew. He would wait in line at the shelter, sometimes an hour or more, for lunch and would enter the lottery for the evening three or four times a week. Initially, he could not put his finger on the deep-seeded emotion lingering inside his gut. He knew this feeling gnawed at him.

On very cold nights the shelter would admit up to thirty additional homeless after the dinner meal was served to those who won the lottery. Those who feared the cold could enter the shelter after 7:00 p.m.; they would be permitted to stay in the cafeteria until 7:00 a.m. A special section was set up for the few women who showed up. Before the thirty left, they were given a cup of coffee and a roll. Those who had won that evening's lottery did not have to leave the shelter until 10:00 a.m. When the evening temperature was going to be too much for Old Man to handle, he would line up outside of the shelter by 5:30 p.m. to make sure he had an indoor place to sleep.

Those days when the temperature was cold but not quite cold enough to open the shelter at 7:00 p.m., Old Man would often join a rather sketchy group of peers under the highway bridge on the other side of Washington Street. He never felt quite safe here, but the others let him bath in the warmth of the fire they would set in a metal trashcan.

Finally, one unusually cool early spring day, he understood the reason for his discomfort. He was humiliated. That was it. It was humiliation. He was humiliated to wait in line hours to eat food he could not pay for. He was humiliated to stand in a long line of men waiting to find out if he would have a place to stay and a dinner to eat. On top of it, he felt guilty as he went into the shelter and watched those whose number was not called munching on their cheese sandwiches. When it was he who wound up with the cheese sandwich, he actually felt less humiliated. There was something energizing about survival.

On this particular day of his new life, Old Man was waiting in line for a beef stew lunch. He had gotten to the shelter around 10:55; so the wait would not be terribly long. He was unusually hungry. Behind him in line was a man nicknamed Prep whom Henry had seen around although he had never talked with him. Why this guy was called Prep, he had no idea.

Henry nodded a distant greeting to Prep who nodded back. Then Prep said, "Hey, man, you want to work a little?"

Henry was surprised to hear anyone say anything about work. He looked at Prep but did not respond.

"Hey, man, you look like a good guy. I have a job this afternoon. It is clearing land. This guy picks me up at 2:00 in a big van and drives me to a field. He says I will get ten dollars an hour."

"That sounds good," said Henry.

"Thing is, my friend can't go. The guy said that he needs both of us. If we both don't show, don't wait for him to pick us up."

Henry still listened, but he was getting closer to the entryway of the shelter.

"So, you want to work for three or four hours? That's thirty or forty dollars cash."

Henry knew that Prep would not have trouble finding a work partner for the afternoon. He was unsure why this stranger had brought up the opportunity to him. "I will have no place to put my suitcase, and I will lose out on the lottery."

"So what, man. Maybe this guy has other jobs at ten dollars an hour, who knows? Maybe you can get off the street. Besides, I got a place where you can put your suitcase. I promise you it will be safe. It's in back of the shelter. There are basement stairs. You can leave it there. Trust me. No one will bother it. I leave stuff there all the time."

So Henry agreed. He thought to himself. "Maybe I have become lazy."

After lunch Henry waited on the corner down the block from the shelter. He was approached by Prep and three other men.

"I thought you had just one friend," Henry said to Jose.

"No, man, I have a few friends. We all work together and make money."

As advertised, a van showed up at 2:00. The five of them got into the van. Once he sat down and the van began moving," Henry became frightened. He had no idea where he was going.

Then, his thoughts turned to his suitcase that he had left at the bottom of the steps next to the entrance to the shelter basement. What if it was gone when he returned? He regretted his decision but it was too late. The van was on the ramp entering the highway.

After a twenty-minute ride, the van stopped next to an open field. In the center of the field was a huge pile of two-by-fours stacked randomly. Henry surmised that there used to be a house on the land and that the new owners were going to build something grander, maybe an apartment building.

The group of five enlistees got out of the van and milled around waiting to hear their assignment although the job was pretty clear. Pick up the wood, put it on the flatbed truck near the pile, and keep going until there was no more wood.

Henry teamed with a muscular, elderly man whom he had seen several times at the shelter. The man said nothing. In rhythm the two would pick up a plank and bring it to the truck. One of the van passengers was on the flatbed helping to stack the pieces of wood. The other recruit carried the smaller pieces of wood to the truck. Prep did nothing. He just watched. Henry wanted to say something, but he decided to keep quiet. After about two hours of hard labor, the driver of the van gave each of the workers a bottle of water. After finishing half of the bottle, Henry went over to Prep and said, "What's the matter. You don't work."

"I am the supervisor," responded Prep with a big smile.

Henry thought about saying more for an instant, but then he thought better. He would just let it be. They couldn't be out here for more than another hour or so.

Finally, the job was done. The group, including Prep, got back into the van that drove them to the shelter. It was almost six o'clock. Henry had missed the lottery and the cheese sandwich. When they got out of the van, the driver handed each worker three five-dollar bills. "Wait a second," said Henry. "I am supposed to get ten an hour. That's thirty-five dollars for three and a half hours work!"

The driver looked at Henry and laughed. "We have to deduct gas and the cost of your refreshments."

Again Henry thought of saying more, but he stopped himself. He looked over at Prep who held two twenty-dollar bills.

Henry went over to Prep. "If you ever say a word to me, ever, I will kill you." Prep could see the anger in Henry's eyes. The supervisor knew it was best to say nothing; without even a smile or a nod, he left.

Henry suddenly thought of his suitcase. He ran around to the back of the shelter. The suitcase was there. It was evident that someone had opened it because the suitcase was lying flat as opposed to being upright against the basement window to the left of the door. Anxiously Henry unzipped the suitcase and went through his belongings. He took an inventory. Only one thing was missing—the hair dryer.

He picked up the suitcase, walked up the stairs, and began rolling it across the sidewalk. His hands and clothes were filthy. The fifteen dollars rested in his left pocket. He did not even think about what to do with his money. All he could think about was changing clothes and getting some of the dirt off of his hands.

"What a bad idea," he mumbled to himself. Henry never worked again.

Soon afterwards, Old Man stopped going to the shelter regularly. Once or twice a month he would enter the lottery hoping to take a shower. Periodically he would give in, however, and wait in line for the noon meal. He saw Prep a few times but decided to say nothing. On very cold nights, he did continue to show up at 5:30 p.m. to stand in line.

As Old Man walked down the street with his suitcase a slight bit lighter, he could only focus on one objective—how to get clean! His hands were filthy from clearing the land. His clothes were covered in dirt. Inside his suitcase he did have another set of clothes, but he did not want to change, even if he found a place of privacy, until he could wash.

Old Man kept wandering. He pulled his suitcase on wheels over the uneven sidewalk. After nearly a half hour, he came upon the bathroom next to the coffee house. On this day, it was remarkably clean. *Must have just been cleaned*, he thought. He looked around. No one was there. So, he felt safe. However, he knew that his time alone was limited.

Old Man went over to the sink on the left because it seemed cleaner. He tried the hot water. Nothing came out. He turned on the cold. He scrubbed his hands using as much soap from the dispenser as he could get in four pushes of the lever. He grabbed a handful of paper towels, wet them, and took off his shirt. As quickly as he could, Old Man washed his upper body. He opened his suitcase and grabbed another shirt that was only slightly worn. Then, came the tricky part. He looked to the door and saw no one. He removed his pants and washed the lower half of his body. "I will count to fifteen," he said aloud. At fourteen he was wiping off his toes. He let the dirty trousers lay on the bathroom floor. He pulled out a wrinkled pair of pants that he had found outside of the Goodwill office the month before.

The entire transformation took only a few minutes. Henry even took out his old toothbrush, which was missing a few bristles, and brushed his teeth. *I wish I had some toothpaste,* he thought.

He looked at the filthy clothes on the floor of the bathroom. "I wish I could wash them," he mumbled. Then, Old Man remembered the fifteen dollars he had in his pocket. *Not only did I get cheated, but now I have to use some of this money to wash clothes.* And that is what Old Man did. He went to the laundromat a few blocks away.

He carried his dirty clothes in one hand and pulled the suitcase with the other. Once there, he decided to wash everything except the clothes he was wearing, whether it smelled badly or not.

· 6 ·

The Disappearing Love

When Old Man was much younger, he was quite good-looking. The ladies often gave him a glare of interest, and he often responded with a slight smile and a sensuous stare. These were the days of three-piece suits and blue blazers. These were the days of Jack Daniels and creamed spinach. These were the days of endless nights with lovely women. These were the days whose reality evaporated. Old Man rarely thought about these times. When he did, his heart lamented and his psyche sloped. He would mumble, "Where did it all go?"

A few days after securing his kite in the treasure trough, Old Man found himself thinking. He was sitting by the fountain where he had made the snowman. He was just sitting there. At first, he was thinking of nothing in particular. Then, he spotted a lovely woman with a spirited bounce in her step; every time she moved, her body bobbed up and down. *She is so alive*, he thought. *Just like Ginny*.

His mind floated. He lost control. He promised himself that he would avoid thinking about the past. Most of the time, he could squelch the glimmer of an image from those days. He could command his mind to stop; it was like an artist who might paint one image in the corner of a canvass and, then, decide to whitewash the canvass. However, this time Old Man could not control the picture his mind painted.

****

"What's your story?" Ginny had asked him.

That one question started it all. Her smile was so pure and her eyes twinkled with delight. But it was Ginny's walk that he now remembered—that bouncy, bouncy of her step. The wonderful optimism that she conveyed! He loved her from the start.

One short talk at Bravado's Pastry Shop led to several. Soon the two of them were almost inseparable. Before he went to work, Ginny would look him in the eye and say, "Henry, I adore you." He would hold her for a moment and say, "I love you from here to Mars." That was their ritual.

When Henry came home, he would sing: "You are the sunshine of my life, and I will always be around you." Ginny would sing the words of the Stevie Wonder song back to him. She would smile with her beautiful eyes that appeared both tame one instant and wild the next. Each look melted his heart.

At work Henry became easily distracted by her almost ghost-like image in his mind. Her smile would appear at the oddest moments. Once, during a presentation about the pros and cons of a possible merger, Henry became hesitant when he imagined Ginny's smile appearing in the midst of a line graph predicting sales increases over the next five years. The center of her mouth encompassed the apex point of the graph. Henry managed to get a hold of himself and finish the presentation with only a few beads of sweat pouring down his neck into the collar of his white shirt.

Henry's twenty-minute drive from his office at the consulting firm to his apartment, where Ginny waited, always seemed to take forever. It was during this drive about nine months into their time together that he first began to wonder. Initially,

Henry dismissed these thoughts as ridiculous. But he couldn't get the idea out of his mind. Then, on the three hundred sixty-first day of their bond, on a Saturday morning, his thoughts turned to concern.

"Darling," he said, "you seem to have bought a lot of clothes lately." He walked over to where she was cooking scrambled eggs. "You look beautiful in them." He paused and swallowed. "I love looking at you in them."

He paused again. Ginny continued to scramble her eggs. She appeared to be listening but was not terribly focused on the conversation. "I know you make OK money. It's just that the clothes must be expensive." He looked at her as she stared at the frying pan. "I will be happy to help you pay for some."

Ginny finished scrambling the eggs. She used the spatula to scrape as much as possible from the pan. When the eggs were on the plate, she turned to Henry. "Thanks, darling. I am alright." And that was that.

That was that until twenty-three days later when Henry and Ginny decided to go to the shopping mall. "While you go look for some shirts," said Ginny, "I am going to go into this store and look for a blouse. We should meet in about a half hour at this spot."

They gave each other a touchy kiss that produced an ever so slight surge of static electricity and went their respective ways.

Henry was not much of a shopper. As he entered a store, he would give himself a time limit. "I am out of here in twelve minutes," he might say. With or without merchandise, he left when time expired. On this day with the men's store crowded, he set his time at fourteen minutes. Henry moved quickly from bin-to-bin grabbing three dress shirts that were the right size and his regular brand. "I am out of here," he mumbled. After paying, he glanced down at his watch. "Record time, nine minutes and fifteen seconds," he bragged to himself. He bolted out of one store to look for Ginny in the other.

Henry looked across the main floor of the department store that was just down the mall from where he bought his shirts. He knew Ginny did not subscribe to his philosophy of exiting before the time-limit alarm goes off. As he entered the store, he tried to guess where she was. He saw a large sign that said "Women's Wear." So he headed in that direction.

Henry wandered past the pleated skirts, the women's suits, and the pants suits. He tried to move about as naturally as possible, feeling a little awkward being the only male in sight. When he arrived at "Lingerie," Henry's anxiety picked up slightly. He actively scouted for Ginny. When he hit the brassiere section, he looked straight ahead. His mind momentarily repeated those childish jokes he used to snicker at. In spite of his immature thoughts, he progressed with a stoic face.

"There she is," he mumbled. Ginny was three aisles in front of him. She did not notice.

Henry thought it would be funny to surprise her. So, he quickly moved to his right in order to circle around and sneak up from behind. He was going to cover her eyes and whisper "surprise" in her ear.

Ginny remained unaware. Henry kept his eyes on her as she meandered through the aisle. Just before turning left to close in on her, he stopped.

Ginny did the unexpected. With the speed of a pro, she removed the tag from one blouse and placed it in her palm. Henry only watched. She walked slowly over to a section labeled "designer boutique." As Ginny moved, she stopped every few feet to hold up a blouse or to feel the material.

Then, Henry gasped. Ginny, operating at warp speed, removed the tag from one blouse in this designer section and replaced it with the tag she had put in her palm. She was good. Someone would have to be focused just on her to catch the switch. Henry suddenly felt very anxious. He had done nothing. But he felt very nervous.

His original plan now defunct, Henry just stood there. "Henry," he heard her shout. "Over here."

Henry slowly walked through the hosiery aisle to Ginny. "Shopping for hose?" she asked. Henry did not respond at first. He told himself to act normally.

"I was circling around to surprise you," he said.

"Look what I found. Look how beautiful this blouse is. Look at the price. $19.95. Can you believe it? This blouse should cost three or four times this."

Henry tried to show moderate excitement. But all he could say was, "Really?"

So, that's how Henry found out how his beloved Ginny could afford her expensive wardrobe. She was good. He was very uncomfortable. He decided to keep his mouth closed and act as if nothing had happened.

The next day, when Ginny went out, Henry couldn't help himself. He had never before looked through her dresser, but now he had to. He wondered how many newly tagged, unworn things he would find.

As Henry started to open the bottom drawer of Ginny's bureau, he remembered how, years before, he and his associates would wager "under and over." They would bet on anything. How many people will vote in the Presidential election? The line is one hundred-twenty million. Are you under or over? How much? How long will it take Bob Friend to come back from the bathroom? What's the line? Usually the first one to shout the line got his way (or her on some occasions—not this one—the three women in the consulting group just rolled their eyes). It was Henry who yelled out: four minutes and forty-five seconds; then, eight grown men wagered how long it would take one of their colleagues to return from the men's room. It was over.

So Henry created a mental "over/under wager" in his mind. "Seven. There will be seven new clothes with tags on them."

He moved to the bureau and opened the first bottom drawer. On the top of the pile he found sweaters that he remembered her wearing. Henry tried to be neat about it because he didn't want Ginny to know that he was surreptitiously going through her personal belongings. He felt a little dirty for doing this. But he was a driven man.

Henry took out each sweater, putting it on the nearby queen-sized bed. He made sure that the order was clear so that he could put the sweaters back in the drawer perfectly.

At the bottom of the first pile of sweaters, he hit pay dirt. He found a cashmere sweater with a large, flowing collar; he looked inside the collar to make sure. He looked at the tag: $29.95. He knew that the idea of buying this sweater for so little was absurd. *But maybe if she were at the right place at the right time*, he thought.

If this were the only one, then he promised himself that he would let it go and hope for the best. He laid the questionable sweater on the bed, making sure to remember that it was at the bottom of the first pile.

In the second of the three piles, he found two more sweaters with tags. In the third, the final pile, he found four blouses; in two of the four cases, he thought the prices of the blouses were ridiculously low even though he knew his knowledge of women's clothes was limited. The other two blouses seemed to be reasonably priced. *I can only guess. I do not spend much time in the women's aisles*, Henry thought to himself.

So, he decided to play detective. *I have to get this thing over with, or I will go crazy,* he said to himself. Henry wrote down as much information as he could about the low-tagged sweaters and the blouses; he would investigate.

After writing the last description, he put everything back into the first bottom drawer and went to the next drawer on the right. This drawer was also deep, and identical in size to the one just searched. Here he found more evidence. One part of him gloated that his suspicions were right. *I am one hell of a detective*, he concluded. But the rest of him became immediately depressed.

In this second drawer he found four newly tagged items. What shocked him most was that some of them were either too small or way too large for Ginny who wore a size seven. There was a rolled-up nightgown, still tagged, that was labeled extra large, which would be big enough for both of them to fit in at the same time. There was a child's blouse with a receipt in the collar, dated eight months ago, that Ginny could not have worn since she was six years old.

Henry didn't even bother to take everything out of this drawer. He just shook his head. He knew that he didn't even need to find out more about the sweaters. The over had won the bet; there were more than seven.

One week later—eight days to be exact—their life together took the first real slide. Ginny came home with an expensive, beautiful sweater. She was very excited. "I am going to try it on for you," she said and let out one of those irresistible smiles that Henry craved.

Henry could no longer control himself. He just blurted out, "Did you change prices on this one, too? Or did you just take it?" Immediately, he knew his error.

Ginny looked at him expressionless. Without missing more than one measure of beats, she responded. "If you must know, I took this one." Her voice was remarkably calm.

Henry tried to respond but couldn't.

"It's a game," Ginny said. "It's a game. It's a rush." She hesitated. "I can tell you don't approve."

"I don't want to see you in jail. I don't want to see us ruined."

"Don't be stupid," she shot back. "I have never gotten caught. Don't you get it? It's the rush. Besides, these stores count on people like me. They build this into the price."

Henry did not answer. He could sense that trouble was ahead.

Ginny could sense it too. "I will stop if you want."

Deep down inside, Henry did not believe her. But he wanted to believe her words. "Please," he told her. Then, he hugged her with more passion than he could remember.

Henry had placed Ginny on a pedestal. To him she was closer to perfect than any woman he had known. He loved her and dreaded what he imagined could happen.

He pushed his anxiety to the back of his mind and struggled to believe Ginny's promise. Perhaps she really did stop. Henry did not see any new clothes since the day of the promise. Five weeks had gone by. He started to relax, and the two of them continued to be in love.

Six weeks later, the inevitable came about. Henry was at work. His cell phone buzzed. These are the words that he remembered from the call. "I've been arrested." He did not have to ask, "for what?"

Lawyer's fees. Probation. Counseling. Ginny appeared to be unaffected. Every morning she continued to say "Henry, I adore you." As usual, he would hold her for a moment and say, "I love you from here to Mars." That was their ritual. Only now his comments seemed less sincere.

He kept repeating to himself, *"When is the next time?"*

Ginny faithfully attended every prescribed counseling session. It was at the fifth session that the counselor asked for Henry to be included. *Maybe, just maybe*, thought Henry. *If she has gotten this far, maybe.*

It was during this session, as he sat next to her on a soft couch, that his "maybe" changed to "doubtful."

Henry asked Ginny if she thought she could really stay away from this problem. "I don't know," she answered. "I miss the rush. I miss it so much."

The counselor asked, "Why?" Henry knew that "why" did not matter.

Two months later, the next inevitable phone call came. "I've been arrested."

Henry cried. He hadn't cried since he was six years old, four days after his mother died. "I'll be there. I'll call the lawyer."

Bail. Prosecution. Admitted guilt. Restitution. Once more, probation with a warning that if this happened again, there would be jail.

Henry knew that there would be a next time. She was addicted. It was a weird type of addiction—one he could never have anticipated, drugs or alcohol maybe, but shoplifting, never.

Old Man sat by the fountain and began to shiver. He had worked so hard to put Ginny in the deepest part of his mind. It hurt too much to think of her. When she left, his heart broke. It never mended. When she left, he began to drink more. Three weeks after she left, he decided to give himself a treat. He knew he had an important meeting, but it was time to do something nice for himself. So, he went into the four-star steak house to have filet mignon, creamed spinach and Jack Daniels.

Old Man smiled. *What would have happened if . . ..* Then, he stopped. No use. No use. His heart was still broken. He still felt the embarrassment that he had the day of the fateful presentation.

He felt a concentrated pain right below his gallbladder every time he thought about how he was the catalyst behind Ginny's leaving. As he stared into space, Old Man shook his head. He mumbled to himself, "How could I have done it?" As he repeated his question over and over his voice became so loud that a couple of passersby began to stare.

About two weeks after the second court appearance, Ginny came home, to their home, with a new shirt. Henry did not ask where she got the shirt or if she had paid for it. He just flew into a rage. He never touched her physically, but his litany of demeaning comments went on and on. At first, Ginny paid little attention. But, the volume of words smothered her. The worst of these words was, "I can't stand you anymore," and "I can't love a thief."

By the end of Henry's destructive commentary, Ginny could not control her tears. But she could control her actions. Without a word, she left. Ironically, Ginny had paid for the shirt. Henry found out when he picked up the receipt from the floor. His tirade immobilized him from running after Ginny. A large piece of Henry's soul died on this day.

It began to snow. Old Man knew he had to find a warmer place for the night. So he brought his mind back to reality. He felt his knees creek as he got up. He tried to straighten up, but he seemed to be fighting gravity. Slowly, he began to move. He did not have to navigate because almost no one was around.

He ambled by the closed pharmacy and was about to turn left. "Are you hungry?" he heard a man's voice say. Old Man looked around. "Are you hungry?" said the middle-aged man, walking with a middle-aged woman. "Would you like half a sandwich? It is left from our dinner. But it is perfectly good."

"Thank you," said Old Man as he grabbed the Styrofoam box containing the sandwich. He smiled at the couple. Once he would have been too proud to take someone else's meal. Now he was grateful.

· 7 ·

The Confrontation

Old Man turned left after the pharmacy into the dark side street heading to find his evening shelter. *I will wait to eat*, he thought. *But I am hungry*, he debated. So he gave in.

He opened the box and gobbled down the half of hamburger and the bonus of a few French fries. He glanced for a place to throw away the container. He made his way to the garbage bin further down the side street.

"I hate you." He heard the words but did not pay much attention.

"I hate you." He heard again. He did not look up. These words could not be for him. He kept his eyes focused on the garbage can.

Old Man heard the words being screamed. "I hate you," the voice said. He turned with a sudden jerk. He looked down the alleyway next to the garbage can.

He tried to make out who was saying these words. He could tell that the voice belonged to a woman—probably a young lady who was alone. He took a couple of steps closer. She was so young and so pretty. She seemed unafraid. "What do you want," she said to Old Man. "Who invited you?"

"I apologize," he responded. "I am sorry. I just wanted to make sure you are OK."

The girl said nothing. He turned to leave. He still hadn't dropped the Styrofoam container in the garbage can. "Don't go," she shouted. "Don't go."

Old Man was taken aback. Those were the last words he expected to hear. At first, he was going to continue on to the trash bin. Something inside made him stay. "No! No," he mumbled partially to the girl and part to himself. He turned around to face the girl. He didn't know what to say. The only thing he could think of was "Hello." He looked down as he talked. He knew this was not the right response.

The girl's eyes reminded him of a deer's soft, penetrating eyes. They were luring with a glimmer of confidence. Old Man struggled to read the girl's eyes. All he could do was to move a step closer, careful not to get too close.

"I am frightened," she finally said. "I am frightened and alone." She paused. "I know you are probably homeless, and I should not be talking to you. But there is something about you that makes me feel safe."

Old Man again struggled to make sense out of this. *The girl is frightened,* he thought, *but she has nowhere to go except to me.* He shivered. *This makes no sense.* He began looking around for a video camera. This had to be part of someone's joke. He suddenly felt used, even abused. He reasoned, *Why would these people make fun of me? I have never harmed them.*

Then, Old Man caught himself. *What if there was no joke? What if the girl really was in trouble?*

"I have no idea how I can help you," he said. "I am at a loss. I have no money."

"I know you think this is some kind of a joke. But it isn't. I am frightened because I am alone. I have little money and even less hope. A voice inside of me told me to find someone to save me. The voice said 'Find the least likely person and you will be OK You will survive."

The girl's soft, deer eyes sparkled. Old Man thought she was mystical, maybe from another world. *If I walk away, I will never know*, he thought. His other conscience dictated, *If I don't walk away, I am going to be sorry*. He wasn't sure if the girl was a goddess or a nut. Either way, he knew his fate.

· 8 ·

The Mystery

Old Man followed the girl. He had no idea why. He just did. There were no signals to stop and reconsider. It was as if an extra-terrestrial force carried him along.

The girl possessed a beauty about her that infatuated him. He just followed her. "We are almost there," she said.

Old Man thought, *Why did she pick me?* In the back of his mind a mantra pounded. *Why am I doing this?* He kept following. She led him through an alley through a doorway and into a garage.

He blindly followed. At the first corner, he almost ran away. At the moment he was about to leave, she turned to him and smiled. "Don't leave me yet," she begged. "Help me for a little while."

"This is where I stay." the girl said. "The house is empty. It is too dangerous to go there. This garage is safe for now."

Old Man asked, "Do you have a home? Why are you here?"

She grabbed his arm gently. "Will you be my savior? Will you save me?"

"Save you! Save you from what? Save you from who?" He was confused. "I can't save myself," he mumbled.

The garage seemed empty, except for a single rake laid against the northern wall and an old wooden stepladder resting nearby. The cement floor promoted a chill. When Old Man looked around again, he noticed a pile of blankets and clothes in the corner to the left of the entrance.

He asked, "How long have you been here?" Before she could answer, he added, "How did you find this?"

The girl only nodded. Old Man had no idea what that meant. "You have to tell me something." He paused. "Or I cannot help you." He paused again. "What is going on?"

Old Man had viewed almost every type of behavior during his many years of homelessness. He had learned to avoid most situations. He knew that getting involved can lead to trouble, even though he never shied away from helping others. It was her deer eyes that had hypnotized his soul and forced him into submission. It wasn't too late to leave.

"I have been here off and on for two months . . . about." She finally admitted.

"I found this place by luck. I was sitting near the fountain on the mall, and I heard the owner telling his friend that he had to leave the area. He had to sell his house right away. He asked his friend if he would look after the house 'til it was sold. He asked his friend to come over to the house to see it. I followed the two of them, just on a hunch."

Old Man still did not understand. "Why did you need to come here? Where were you living?"

The girl began to get angry. She started to grit her teeth. Her soft, eyes narrowed.

"I am sorry if I intruded. I won't ask again." He apologized.

"It is not your fault. I brought you here to this garage." The girl's stomach muscles tensed. Her whole body seemed to shake slightly. "I came to town two years ago to be with my boyfriend. His name was Gregory. I say 'was' because he is dead."

Old Man stood silently in the cold garage. The only light came from a streetlamp outside the garage door.

"He was a great person. I loved him so much. We did not have much money, but, as they say in the movies, we were happy." The girl looked down. "Gregory was from a rich family. One year before I came here to be with him, his parents were killed in an automobile accident. It turned out there wasn't as much money as Gregory's two brothers thought. They had counted on millions and the lawyer told them there was only several thousand. So, the brothers figured out a way to cheat Gregory out of his share. It wasn't really that much. But it would have helped."

The girl sat down on the cement floor. Her shoulders drooped. It was like a vacuum tube had sucked some of the air out of her.

"You say 'It would have helped,'" interjected Old Man.

"Yes, Gregory became very sick. Everything we had—not very much–went for bills. Gregory refused to contact his brothers or any relatives. He was too proud. I should have called them. Soon he died."

Old Man didn't know what to think. He still kept asking himself, *Why am I here?*

"I have crawled inside myself since Gregory died. I had no interest in working and no money. I just wanted to be at peace. I talk to Gregory every night. Tonight I told him that I hated him. He knows it is not true."

"Then, I saw you at the fountain. It was at the same fountain that I overheard the men talking about this house. You were making a snowman. You were so kind with that boy. You made me smile. You were the kindest person I had ever seen."

Old Man felt warm inside. No one had ever called him kind. He didn't think of himself as kind.

"So," she continued, "I have been following you. Not every minute. But you go to the fountain almost every day. I wait for you, sometimes. Tonight I had to talk with you. I need someone I can trust. I am dying inside, and I am too young for that to happen."

· 9 ·

The Moment of Guilt

When Henry was an early teen, Freddy Martin used to follow him around. Freddy had no friends and desperately wanted to be friends with him. One day Henry had enough and ordered poor Freddy to stay away. "I don't want to be your friend," he told the lonely boy. "Stay away." Freddy never bothered Henry again. One year later Freddy hanged himself. Old Man still felt secretly responsible.

Now, with this strange girl who attached herself to him, Old Man's mind spawned images of Freddy Martin. These images dictated his conclusion that he could not leave this girl alone. Not just yet anyway.

Old Man asked the girl, "What do you want to do?"

"I have to escape," she said. "I have to get out of here."

"What stops you?"

"I feel trapped. I can't move forward. It's like I keep falling into a deeper hole. Every day it seems harder and harder. I need help."

The girl's story seemed incomplete. But Old Man could not break away from some kind of chemical bond that pushed him into submission.

He knew it was not the right moment to bring up counseling. Besides he still remembered how well counseling had worked with his beloved Ginny.

He could see that she trusted no one, except maybe him. He had learned on the street to trust no one, but deep down inside he did trust most people. Of course, Hungry Harry was an exception.

Old Man looked at the corner of the garage where there were blankets in a pile. He pointed and asked, "Do you sleep there?"

"Some nights. When I can, I sneak into the house to use the bathroom. I wait until two or three in the morning and try not to make any noise. I know it is a matter of time 'til I get caught."

Old Man was exhausted. "Can you spare a blanket?" The girl looked at him quizzically. "I need to sleep. Is that OK? In the morning we will decide what to do."

And so it was. Old Man wrapped himself in one of the blankets and fell asleep on the concrete floor of the garage. He dreamt that Freddy Martin was wrapped in a blanket next to him. Freddy smiled at Henry and mouthed the words "good job."

As for the girl, she sat up and stared at her savior as he slept. She prayed for the safety of both of them. She carefully put one of the blankets under Old Man's head and kissed his forehead. Then she moved to the other side of the garage and curled into one blanket while placing the other one under her head.

The night was not especially frigid. So, the garage floor was not as cold as it had been. The mice and chipmunks stayed outside; no need to seek refuge in the garage.

Old Man woke up. There was a little daylight. He figured it was about 6:30. He turned over to stare at the girl who was four or five feet away. He smiled. Maybe he could help her. He couldn't handle another Freddy Martin, not at this time in his life.

He thought, *If I am not going to make this happen, I have to go now.*

He sat up. She was still asleep. He could go, and he would be off the hook. When he saw her again near the fountain, he would just tell her, "I am too old and tired to help you." But he stayed. He continued to watch her sleep, trying to figure why he couldn't leave and what to do.

He wasn't sure what she wanted or what she needed. His mind was confused. Snap out of it, he ordered his mind. He thought back to a time when he solved problems every day; to a time when he made a good deal of money; to a time when he had no difficulties making up his mind. He could do this again. But he did not understand her problem.

In one sense he actually was excited. Most of his life during this past decade had been based on him creating a path for his own survival. Now, he could trace a path for someone else. Why not?

During those prosperous times, so many years ago, Henry had been generous. His colleagues were never really pals, but they would come to him with their problems. He would always listen and try to help. He never resented his role.

· 10 ·

The Ghosts of Hope

Once he even saved a marriage. Elaine Markinger, who worked with Henry on a few select mergers, was having trouble in her marriage. She told him that she loved her husband, but that he seemed distant. Henry listened for nearly an hour as Elaine revealed how her marriage was falling apart. He just listened. This was Henry's best trait. He can sit for long, long stretches and just listen. Most people would need to ask a question or take a break or make an excuse and leave. Henry could stay focused until the person was finished or too exhausted to continue.

After listening, he only made one simple suggestion. "Go home. Bring him a dozen roses with a card telling him you love him. Then, tell him you want to work through whatever is getting in the way." Henry added, "If he feels like you do, then work together to find someone professional to talk to. You will know that if it doesn't work, you did whatever you could."

Elaine Markinger listened to her peer's advice. She brought home a dozen roses. Wrote a card. Talked with her husband. Went to a therapist. The couple was still married years later while Old Man roamed the streets. "I could save her marriage, but not Ginny," he sadly mumbled to himself.

Thinking of Elaine pushed Old Man's thoughts to his colleagues from those prosperous times. Maybe they could help him now. He didn't want help for himself, just for the girl.

He thought out loud, "Maybe if it's money she needs, I can ask some people I knew in the past. Maybe they will help. Maybe I can borrow one or two hundred dollars from three or four people. Maybe that would not be enough to get her a new start."

Old Man would never borrow money for himself from a former colleague. About six months ago, he ran into Arnie Yolanda who looked like his successes had stayed with him throughout the years. At first, Old Man tried to hide from Arnie who was walking straight for the fountain on a warm spring day. Old Man had been taking advantage of the weather, sitting quietly on the stone border of the fountain. He looked even worse than usual; he had not slept much over the past few days. (One night stray cats kept crisscrossing his path as he lay on a patch of grass at the edge of the public park. Last night a police officer woke him up from a deep sleep to tell him he had to move on.)

So, when Old Man saw Arnie, he hoped that his former colleague would not recognize him. He did not feel ashamed of what he had become until he was confronted by someone who knew what he had been.

"Henry, is that you?" asked Arnie. Old Man just nodded. "Can I help?" asked Arnie. Old Man nodded "no." Arnie asked again, and he again shook his head "no." After a second thought, Arnie said, "Here is my card. Let me know if I can help." Old Man was relieved that the humiliation was over.

Arnie started to leave. He stopped and turned again. "Are you sure, Henry?" Old Man quietly shook his head. "I remember how you stayed that night in the bar. You had one hell of a left hand." Even Old Man smiled at this.

"It was one hell of a fight," Old Man responded.

"Henry, I am worried about you." Arnie reached into his wallet. He randomly pulled out several denominations of money. "At least let me give you this." Arnie paused. "You can pay me back when things get better." Arnie hesitated. "Or, when you can."

Old Man, again, shook his head. "You have to promise me you will call," Arnie added. He gave Arnie a narrow smile.

He, again, looked at the girl while she slept. But with the girl, it would be different. He would help her. Old Man would figure out how to see Arnie and a couple of his old colleagues and ask for money. Not for himself, but for this unusual girl that seemed to need him; the girl he couldn't leave. His head seemed ready to explode. *Help her do what?* He continued to watch her as she slept. Just as a father would, he tried to imagine what she would become.

Then, Old Man thought back to the night in the bar with his old colleague.

Arnie Yolanda had a terrible temper. He could get angry over the most absurd of events. Once he got livid when his assistant forgot to put the meeting notes in the center of his desk; they were placed in the corner. "Damn it! I am paying you to be precise. I want you to put those notes exactly where I tell you." Ironically, Arnie was not too precise himself. Henry was constantly finding errors in Arnie's calculations and typos in his writing.

But underneath it all, Arnie had a heart. Old Man remembered how every year Arnie would dress as Santa Clause, parading from homeless shelter to homeless shelter bearing gifts that he purchased with his own money. Even now, many years later, he had fond memories of his colleague.

Once Henry and Arnie had gone out for a drink at a local pub. They wound up standing next to three cocky, young executives from a rival firm. The three began making disparaging comments to Arnie and Henry. Arnie called it "trash talking." Henry called it "comments to be ignored." Henry let the comments go. Arnie wouldn't. "Did your mothers teach you to be rude bastards, or did you learn it on your own," retorted Arnie to the three. Before long, Henry was in the middle of fight that he wanted to avoid. But friendship is friendship. Maybe honor is honor.

Besides, Henry knew how to fight. He learned growing up in his neighborhood. Bo Watkins, the neighborhood bully, had taken a strong disliking to Henry. "I don't like you," Bo had proclaimed. Henry didn't respond. "I am going to beat you up," said Bo. "So give me a quarter, or I'll beat you up." Henry had never fought before this moment with Bo, the bully. He had watched wrestling and boxing on T.V., but he had never been in a real fight.

Now Henry had a choice. He decided he would defend his honor. He knew this kid would be back every day for a quarter. He had no choice. So, before Bo Watkins could rear back for a punch, Henry assembled as much energy as he could muster. He tried to infuse his body with the spirit of Rocky Marciano, who was his father's idol. With all his might, he aimed right for the nose and socked the bully right in the little valley above the cheekbone next to the nose. To Henry's surprise, he had gotten a bull's eye—Bo Watkins would have a black eye and a broken nose.

All the bully could say between uncontrollable tears was, "You sucker punched me." Word got around, and no one messed with Henry. This was Henry's last fight until that moment with Arnie in the bar.

At that moment in the bar, Henry called up the ghost of Bo Watkins and summoned the spirit of "The Rock" once again. With unpredictable energy the punches landed. Arnie waved to his friend when he saw that he was not to be abandoned. On the way out of the bar, two hundred dollars poorer (that was the compromise with the bar tender to avoid the police), he said to his colleague, "That's the last time I am going out drinking with you."

Old Man smiled at his memory.

The girl was still sleeping. His mind kept drifting to the past. "Arnie Yolanda," he murmured. He remembered that Arnie was the last person he saw on his way out the corporate door. He remembered it was a cold day, colder than he anticipated. He did not bother wearing his warmer coat. He remembered the chill that hit him when he walked out of the lobby elevator into the cold. He remembered trying to fit the cardboard box filled with his belongings into the revolving door. He remembered thinking: *This is stupid, I should have gone through the push door.*

He remembered being so angry that he did not want to ask the security guards escorting him out of the building for help.

Old Man lay down on one blanket and rested his head on the second blanket that the girl had placed under his head. He could not sleep again. His mind was racing. He saw himself as he exited the revolving door and moved into the cold. His first thought was to take that cardboard box filled with his "treasures" and dump it in the nearest trashcan. But he didn't. He carried the box to his Audi and drove to his empty apartment.

Ginny had left three months before he was fired. She left a note. "I love you. I always will love you. I wish we could be together forever. But I know it is not in the stars. I have to go. I am sorry. Love, Ginny."

Henry understood, but he didn't want to understand. His life had gone from contented order to an empty form of chaos. He took the picture of Ginny from the cardboard box and held it between his hands. His heart ached. He felt abandoned.

This was the same feeling, the same exact emotion that almost brought him down as a youth. His mother was rarely there, and his father sometimes tried but didn't know how to parent most of the time.

Word of Henry's successful knockout punch of the bully got around. Pretty soon every undesirable youth in school sought him out. "Let's form a gang," some would say. "Let's beat the crap out of that kid over there. He thinks he's so great because his parents are rich." Henry was tempted but violence was not really part of his makeup.

Yet, he kept hanging out with these kids. They seemed to be the closest thing he had to a family. So, young Henry was on the brink. "I should have wound up in jail," Old Man mumbled to himself as he reflected.

· 11 ·

The Event

But one event changed everything. One Sunday afternoon his father was sober which was a rarity. His mother had died five years before. Old Man thought of the words his father said. "Henry, I found this kite. Let's go fly it."

This moment changed everything. The excitement; the two of them together; the two of them laughing; the kite going up and up. Henry, for the first time, understood what it meant to be optimistic—to hope, to see beauty and grace.

From that instant on, Henry was transformed. He abandoned his rowdy friends. Henry and his father never flew a kite again. But that one moment changed him into what he became until that day when he walked out of the revolving door with a cardboard box and into an apartment without Ginny.

· 12 ·

One Punch Too Many

Old Man was not asleep. His mind was perked up. Thinking about the note from Ginny regurgitated deep-seeded emotions that he had not realized in years. At first, sadness; then, a sense of anger – this was like the anger that filtered his actions in the months following the note.

Henry had not been an angry person. Even when he punched the bully, he did not feel a great surge of anger. If he had, he would have punched him again. Henry sought peace. That was really what he wanted. Unfortunately, any semblance of inner peace was shattered.

In the months after Ginny left, every day moments brought about a surge of anger. If someone pushed him accidentally, Henry took it as an affront and pushed back. If a line was too long, he would exclaim, "Come on, let's go." Patience was a forgotten virtue.

A couple of months before being fired from his job, Henry decided that getting out, even for a cup of coffee, would be a good idea. So, he ventured down the block to what was his favorite café hideaway, even though he hadn't been there in a while. Henry bought a newspaper and a cup of dark roast coffee. He found a small table near the back of the café to sit. There he spent the next twenty minutes reading the paper and drinking his coffee. Henry had not been more relaxed in a while.

After finishing his first cup of coffee, Henry brought his cup to the main counter to purchase a refill. Before leaving the table, he carefully slid the newspaper under the collar of his coat that was on the back of his chair. *No one is going to think this is left over*, he thought.

When he returned to his table with the refill, Henry noticed that the newspaper was gone. He looked around the floor, but it was not there. He put his coffee on the table, glancing to his right. There he saw a middle-aged man reading the same newspaper that he had purchased.

"Excuse me," Henry said to the middle-aged man. "Did you happen to get that newspaper from my chair?"

The man looked up. "What about it?"

"Well, that's my newspaper," Henry said.

"I'll give it back when I'm done," responded the man.

Henry felt a rage build up. In previous times he might have given it one more go round of reasoning. Not this time. Henry quickly reached out. He snapped the paper out of the hands of the middle-aged man, adding the word "asshole" to the action.

The man reached to grab the paper back. Henry's rage resuscitated the spirit of "The Rock." The same left hand that found the little well above Bo, the bully's, cheekbone smashed into the jaw of the middle-aged man.

Henry feeling triumphant did not run. He sat back down to read his paper that he reclaimed fair and square. He did not notice the crowd that gathered around the middle-aged man nor the police officer that approached his table.

Henry's perception that he was the victim was not shared by the officer nor by the customers who only witnessed part of the action.

Old Man shook his head. He no longer felt this surge of anger. He did feel regret. "I wish it didn't happen," he mumbled softly. "I wish it didn't happen."

But it did. Ironically, Henry wound up at the same police station where Ginny had been. "You look familiar," one of the officers at the front desk said.

Lawyer's fees. Probation. And counseling. The drill that Henry knew all too well. Oh, there was one other result. The lawsuit: the lawsuit that was settled out of court.

By the end, Henry was nearly broke. That cup of coffee turned out to be very expensive.

· 13 ·

The End of the Line

Old Man almost fell back asleep. He was drifting off. Suddenly, he heard the deep bark of a dog that startled him. He opened his eyes. The girl was still sleeping. He had no idea what time it was. He knew it was light enough to be near sunrise.

He heard the dog again. The girl did not move. He could hear her breathing normally; so he knew she was ok. His mind focused on the dog's deep throaty bark. The last time he remembered hearing that sound was years ago right after he his infamous Jack Daniels and creamed spinach moment.

A week after the Jack Daniel's incident, his boss called him upstairs to let him know that he was out. "I talked with McGee about your presentation last week. He said you seemed," the president paused, "you seemed a little out of sorts," He paused again. "And you had food, McGee said 'tufts of food' stuck between your teeth!"

Henry did not say anything. He had tried to block the incident from his mind. No one had said anything for several days. So, Henry had figured all was forgotten. He realized he was wrong. Mr. Ciecle was calling him in for a reprimand, or worse.

"Henry, you have done pretty good work over the years. I think we have paid you fairly. I am going to have to let you go."

Henry looked at the president of the consulting firm. "I may have screwed up. I am sorry. I have been going through some tough times. But I have made this firm a lot of money. I need another chance." In the back of Henry's mind was a cash register showing debits and balances. He counted on his salary to pay off his debts. He needed the money. He was no longer enamored by the work. In fact, before the incident, he had been thinking of changing jobs anyway.

"Henry, we lost McGee who was our second biggest client. You know how it works."

"Don't my years of success here count for anything?" Henry stared at this boss. He was no longer humbled, creamed spinach or not.

"If you must know your work during this past year has been less than stellar. For the past twelve months, we have been carrying you." Ciecle reached into his drawer. "Here is your performance evaluation for the past year." He handed it to Henry.

Henry looked over the report. He became increasingly angered with words like "slacking" and "negative client reaction" and "uncooperative."

Henry had sworn to himself that he would control his temper. He was already in financial trouble. Yet, he couldn't control an inner buildup of rage that enveloped his organs, moving through his chest into his neck defying gravity and propelling his left arm into an upward recoil.

Without warning, Henry stood. He briefly stared at Mr. Ciecle. Albert as he used to call him, moved two steps behind the shiny, oak desk that now separated them and sat down. Trying to look busy, Albert nervously reached across the pile of papers on the desk (making sure not to strike the Tiffany desk light or the statue resting to his left).

While summoning up "The Rock," Henry took better aim than he had at the coffee house. Mr. Ciecle, Albert, flew out of his chair onto the floor. Henry just stared at him. Henry knew that this was a mistake, a worse mistake than at the coffee house. He knew that his days at a high-priced consulting firm were over. "Another lawsuit," he mumbled. Mr. Ciecle did not hear Henry's comment through the melody of his moaning.

Henry thought briefly of apologizing. He thought about going over and helping his former boss. But he subliminally rejected both ideas. He just watched Ciecle roll around near the chair for a moment. Then, he, with a surprisingly calm demeanor, walked out of the president's office and told Ms. Jenkins, the executive secretary, "I think you are going to need some ice."

Henry walked through the row of less important assistants and through the glass door that led to the elevators to the second floor where his office was. There he looked around and fortunately found a cardboard box that had contained office supplies a few feet away. He rapidly placed his belongings in the box.

Just when he was about finished, two security guards, Carl and Glenn, showed up. "We have to get you out of here, Henry. There is a lot of shit coming down," said Glenn. Fortunately for Henry, he had always been nice to these guys. He always had asked about their families and had bought them bottles of expensive Bourbon at Christmas time. So, the security guards did their job, but they cut Henry slack. They were as concerned about getting him safely out of the building as getting him out of the offices.

So, Henry made his way through the revolving door. He had crossed the final path from comfortable to survival.

Henry's job was gone. He was too disheartened to even think of applying for unemployment compensation. Worst of all, he had no one to go home to. His heart was haunted by an echo of despair. *Where had it all gone wrong?*

· 14 ·

Running from the Truth

Old Man lay there on the dusty blanket. He thought, *How did it go wrong?* He looked over at the girl who continued to sleep, even though she had turned over. She must not have slept for days,

He heard the dog bark again. His mind created the image of a large barking Labrador as it quickly retreated down the alleyway between Buster's Computer Store and Dally's Pawn Shop. Old Man saw Henry not turning around. Henry kept moving, making a quick exit, dodging streams of people with shopping bags. Nowadays, these people with shopping bags would do all they could to dodge the homeless-looking Old Man. Back then, Henry had not quite devolved in the undesirable he had become. Ginny had been gone for only a little while.

I was walking near the fountain, almost broke, he thought. *I looked like hell. I hadn't worked in almost a year,* his mind said. "Then, I saw her," he mumbled to himself. He saw Ginny. She was across the street. She looked so beautiful. She looked radiant. Henry wanted to run to her, but he was ashamed. He looked so unkempt. During the previous several months he had gone from his luxury apartment to one room in the basement of a decrepit building. His money was virtually gone. He knew he would be on the street soon.

Henry received no severance from his job. He received the message that if he tried to apply for unemployment, Ciecle would file battery charges against him. He was lucky he didn't have to face another lawsuit. Mr. Ciecle told Henry's former associates that if any of them was seen with that "angry ingrate, I will fire you on the spot." He added, "If anyone tries to give him money, you will be fired." So no one called or helped Henry; no one dared.

He had tried to get a job. At first he went to competing consulting firms. No one would see him. He tried to contact a "headhunter" who just two years prior had promised to match Henry to a new job that paid nearly double. He wished he had accepted. Maybe things would have been different. Deep down inside, Henry didn't seem to care if he worked or not. He had little or no motivation. He couldn't even bring himself to ask for a job at a fast-food restaurant.

So, his money was nearly gone. His personal appearance was questionable. He had given up shaving a couple of months earlier. He had sold those clothes that were worth selling to a second-hand clothing shop and was left with three shirts, two sweaters, three pairs of pants, one coat, and some underwear that no one wanted to buy and a hair dryer. "When it is time to go, I will pack it all in one suitcase," he mused.

Over time Old Man's one suitcase had become a shopping bag; his shopping bag had become his security blanket. He did have an old, small airline blanket tucked in the bag. But this Virgin Airline reject served as his pillow; it offered no security. Old Man thought of the treasures that he kept tucked away in the well next to the apartment building as his retirement fund. In the olden days, he had well over fifty thousand dollars in his fund. After the lawsuit, most of that disappeared. Now his only savings were his stash in the well. These treasures were sacred. Since he added his kite, they were even more sacred.

But his shopping bag was different. This contained his survival and his amusement. Inside was what he found and what he wanted to hold onto. At any moment there could be a little food, a book that he found in the trash, a recent newspaper, an extra pair of socks, a sweater or a pen. When one shopping bag became too ripped or torn, Old Man would go into Green's Supermarket. He would look for Lucille who worked one of the registers. She would slip him a new paper shopping bag with two attached handles.

Lucille had taken a liking to Old Man. She had seen him on the street and had stopped to talk with him on several occasions. Once in a while she would tell him to meet her in front of Green's at the end of her shift. She would give him a sandwich and a drink. Old Man was never sure if Lucille paid for these herself. He was grateful and always said "thank you." Each time he took the food, he would tell Lucille, "When I strike it rich, you will be the first on my list." Lucille would smile. She was the only person who would give him a kiss on his cheek.

Sometimes, Old Man would look for paper in the trash. He would sit by the fountain or in a park and write poetry – nothing significant, just for his own amusement.

One cold, winter day, months after his return to the steak house, he was shivering. With his hand shaking, he reached into his shopping bag and pulled out a pen. He spotted a piece of crumbled up paper in the trash. One side of the paper contained a listing of directions; the other side was blank. So, the Old Man wrote.

> I am shivering out here.
> Too cold for a beer
> Maybe a shot on ice
> Would taste real nice.

He smiled at his poem. His verse did create a craving for a shot of Jack Daniels. "Why not," he thought. He walked to the street corner of Main and Morrison and began reading his poem to passersby. After he finished each reading, he took his scraggly hat off of his head and held it out for any donation. He repeated this process over and over. Old Man only begged for money at selected times, times when he wanted something. At this moment, he wanted a shot of Jack Daniels. After thirty-two repetitions of his poem, he had enough savings to buy three shots of Jack Daniels on sale a block away at Felder's Liquor Store for two dollars and thirty cents a shot. He asked Felder for three mini-bottles of Jack Daniels as he put the money on the counter. "By any chance do you have a paper cup you could spare?" Mr. Felder stared at him. "It is barbaric to drink straight out of a bottle," continued Old Man. Mr. Felder sighed, reached under the counter and gave him a small paper cup.

Old Man placed his three tiny bottles of Jack Daniels in his shopping bag along with the paper cup. He retreated to a quiet bench on a side street with little traffic. He took one of the three bottles out of the bag, opened it, and poured the contents into the paper cup. For a few minutes, he felt young and prosperous. *If I only had some creamed spinach,* he thought.

Here he was near the fountain sipping from the paper cup filled with the first mini of Jack. Across the way he again saw Ginny. Oddly, she was pushing a baby carriage. He stood and strained his neck to get a look inside the carriage. He calculated the months. Two years had gone by. The baby in the carriage looked to be about a year old. He was sure it wasn't his child. Ginny had found someone else. "It didn't take her long," he commented to himself.

When Ginny started across the plaza towards Henry, he jumped up and ducked into the alleyway, dropping his paper cup which was still half full. He was desperately trying to avoid her. Henry felt ashamed at what he had become—a disheveled human being who now looked so unappealing.

He heard Ginny yell, "Henry. Please stop. I want to talk to you. Henry wait." But he kept going. Soon she gave up and retreated back to the other side of the plaza. After a little while of hiding in the shadows, Old Man sneaked back to make sure she was gone.

He was determined to make sure that Ginny never saw him again. He avoided the fountain area for several weeks. Old Man never knew that Ginny returned there every day for a month, hoping to see him. Then, she gave up.

Old Man did not see Ginny again for nearly fourteen years. She was walking with another woman and a girl who must have been about fifteen or sixteen. Maybe this was her daughter grown up.

Old Man shook his head. "Maybe I should have waited," he mumbled aloud. "I couldn't let her see me like that." He paused. "I couldn't let her see me now."

· 15 ·

The Set Up

He looked over at the girl. She was still sleeping. *If she isn't up soon, I am going to wake her*, he thought. *I must go. I can't help her. I can't even help myself*, he added.

Suddenly, Old Man heard a doorbell ring. He wasn't sure if the sound came from the house that accompanied the garage or the neighboring one. At any rate, he became frightened. He didn't want to get discovered in the garage. And with a young girl! He heard footsteps. They were getting louder. Then, he heard a man's voice say "Not home. We will call later. We can try to deliver it tomorrow." The running car or truck engine got quieter until there was no sound.

"Safe for now," he said aloud. "I should wait 'til she gets up. I am going to wake her in five minutes." Old Man laughed. He thought to himself, *How will I know when it is five minutes?*

The fear he felt from hearing the doorbell reminded him of a similar feeling. *Unfortunately, I wish that never happened,* thought Old Man. *That was the stupidest I have ever been.*

Henry had been without an apartment for several months. He was finding life on the street to be difficult and unrewarding. He had passed the "no return" square. No place to live; no job; no interest in getting a job. But he was worried. He had not yet learned to really survive. Fortunately, the time of year was late spring. At least, he had the warmer weather although the evening was still cold enough to represent a challenge to his creativity. Henry was an amateur in a high-level professional game. He occasionally talked with some of his new colleagues. But these conversations were brief. Henry was intimidated by their gruff strength of character. *I am not this tough*, Henry admitted to himself. *I am not sure if I can make it here.*

During this time of doubt, Henry had discovered that if he put his blanket on the street side of Liney Park's landscaping that no one would bother him. It was an unusually warm, sunny day. Henry's anxiety was drowned out by the sheer power of a perfect early afternoon. He looked around and saw three of his colleagues spread around the area. The park was filled with mothers and nannies watching their children run to and from the playscape.

Henry found a small patch of grass behind the box hedges. He was well enough hidden. He lay down on his blanket and faced the warm sun. He did not initially reminisce. His mind just wandered. As he lay there, he started to think of other sunny days. He remembered the special moments in Aruba with Ginny when all was good. He remembered flying the kite with his father. He remembered Stan Aranci's funeral. He asked, *Why did I think of that? I am so ashamed.*

Henry had worked with Stan Aranci who was a world class "nice guy." Stan was not going to set the world on fire, but his heart was always in the right place. How Stan got appointed as unit director even the gods couldn't figure out. He was a nice guy, but he was not the brightest light in the group. But, in fairness, he was competent.

Henry's colleagues at the consulting firm thought of Stan as a dolt. Henry was really the only one who went out of his way to be supportive of Stan. The others mocked their unit director.

One snowy late spring morning, Billy Johnstone, another of Henry's colleagues, summoned his minion of immature but very bright fellow stars to his desk. "Hey, look at this." A friend of Billy Johnstone's had emailed him some unthinkable pictures showing sexual intimacy between adults and minors.

The other members of the group were both appalled and intrigued. "You better get rid of that stuff now," one colleague told Billy. "Those are against the law," said another.

Billy was about to erase the email when he stopped. "Let's forward these to Stan. He will go crazy," said Billy. So, the group figured out a way to route the obscene pictures to Stan's computer without evidence being traced back to one of their computers.

"We'll tell him it was a joke. Just let him sweat for a while," concluded Billy.

Stan opened the obscene pictures. He was beside himself. Stan was about to erase the pictures when Mr. Ciecle happened to walk by. He took one look at Stan's computer screen and went quietly berserk. He grabbed Stan's computer and ordered Stan off of the site, never to return.

Henry was not part of this fiasco. He knew nothing about it until he saw Stan in shock walking out. Henry asked, "What happened?" At first, no one responded with any specifics. Then, one of the minion spilled the beans.

"You have to go up to Ciecle now and tell him what happened. Tell him what you guys did. This is someone's life."

The follower looked shocked. "If I go up there now, what do you think will happen to me. This will blow over in a day or two."

Henry made his way to Mr. Ciecle's office. His assistant stopped him from entering. "The police are in there. You can't go in," she said.

"I have to," said Henry. "I know what really happened."

"Mr. Ciecle left strict orders he is not to be disturbed under any circumstance."

"I need to see him."

"How about in two hours at 1:00, right after lunch," the assistant replied.

When Henry appeared at 1:00 to see Ciecle, the president of the consulting firm was nowhere to be found. "Unfortunately, he went out and won't be back until morning," the assistant said. "I can reschedule you for 9:00."

As Henry lay on the old blanket thinking of this tragic episode in his life, he subtly shook his head. "I waited," he mumbled. "How stupid! I am responsible. I should have banged on his door and made him let me in."

In the time between Mr. Ciecle going out for the day and the 9:00 a.m. meeting, Stan Aranci killed himself. Stan left work in shock. On his way home, he stopped at the gun store and bought a .45 with six bullets. He only needed one.

Stan Aranci's funeral was on a warm spring day like this one. After he was buried, Henry cried for hours.

The morning following the incident Henry did see Mr. Ciecle at 9:00. He told him what he knew about the pornography. The entire minion was fired. Mr. Ciecle continued to pay Stan's salary to Stan's widow who had to explain what happened to her three elementary-aged children.

Billy Johnstone was prosecuted for sending pornography. His worst nightmare was being placed on the child predator list.

Old Man stared at the girl. *I can't be part of this again. I have to help her*, he concluded. He wanted to wake the girl, but his mind returned to the park. He was laying on the old blanket feeling momentarily secure.

Old Man felt the warmth of the rising sun coming through the window in the garage. He closed his eyes and recalled a time when he had only been on the street a little while. The picture he saw was that of himself looking years older than his real age. He became melancholy. *I seemed to have aged so much.*

Then, again, he thought about the day in the park before he crowned himself Old Man. He remembered himself laying on the blanket. As he lay on the blanket next to an elm tree, he heard a low-pitched voice quietly saying, "You are new here." Old Man recalled looking to his left and up. The body behind the voice was lanky. The man had a scraggly beard but his clothes seemed better than the normal hand-me-downs on the street. Oddly, the man had both an old suitcase, about the size of the one Henry was dragging around at the time, and a leather briefcase, which was most unusual.

"Yes," replied Henry. The strange man sat down next to him. He was startled. In a knee-jerk response, Henry sat up.

"Beautiful day, eh?" said the man. Henry nodded. He had learned not to say too much to anyone. "How you doin' for money?" asked the man.

Henry did not respond. He had nothing to give. In fact, all he had was the three dollars in change he had begged and the quarter he had found on the grass near the bush.

"I'm not asking you for money. I want to know if you need money," said the man.

Henry still remained silent. He remembered the one lesson his father had taught him: "If it sounds too good to be true, it is."

"Listen, if you are not interested, just nod your head," said the man.

Henry nodded his head, and the man left. *That should have been the end of it,* said Old Man to himself. But it wasn't. As fate, or bad luck, would have it, Henry again ran into this same man a month later during a violent thunderstorm. For protection from the storm, he hid under the overhang along the side of Peeve's Food Store. He was not alone. There was an odd mixture of cultures seeking protection; men in expensive business suits; mothers with their baby carriages; kids on their way home from school; and a few people of the street. The area under the overhang was crowded. Usually, people would keep their distance from him and the unmistakable odor that accompanied his lifestyle. But at this moment, no one seemed to care. All anyone wanted was protection.

Henry saw the man with the low voice standing next to him; he nodded but did not say anything. The deviant man did the same, and quickly started to run through the pouring rain and down the side of the road. Henry lost sight of him.

Then, Henry saw three soaked police officers running up to the crowd of people still under the overhang. One of the officers yelled to the crowd still bunched together. "Have you seen a male, about 5 feet 8 inches, thin with a scraggly beard, wearing a green coat?" One voice nearby answered, "He was right up there," pointing to Henry's location. "He ran away a minute ago. He ran that way," said the Good Samaritan pointing down the side street. The three officers, soon to be even more waterlogged, took off in pursuit. Henry watched them slog down the flooded street.

When the rain finally stopped, Henry grabbed his suitcase containing some clothes and a comb and other essentials, and his shopping bag. He began the trek to find a reasonable dry spot to settle in for the day. He meandered down several little streets and finally came to a large garbage bin in back of Stop & Save Food Store.

The bin was about six feet tall. Henry thought for a moment, then acted. He put down his suitcase. With his shopping bag placed over his right wrist, he used his might to prop himself up over the edge of the bin where the cover was folded back. At first, his attempts to pull himself over the lip of the bin failed. Finally, he realized that a running start could provide his body with a much-needed boost. With one leg over the top of the garbage bin he could look inside.

"Treasures!" he proclaimed. There was a nest egg of outdated food that the store workers had discarded. Henry could see at least five neatly-wrapped sandwiches, some oranges, a few cucumbers, and a few loaves of bread.

Henry had gone into dumpsters before. He hoped to reach his food without having to commit to a jump or dive inside the dumpster. With one arm, he held the shopping bag open and with the other he reached for the bounty.

Unfortunately, the food was out of reach. So, Henry, reticently pushed himself over the top of the garbage bin. After a brief pause, he jumped inside. The smell was not the best, but the reward was worth unpleasantness. As he spilled into the bin, he lost control of his shopping bag and some of its content tumbled out. He watched some of the clothes from the bag fall into the bin. With a bit of effort, he righted the bag before everything fell out and then replaced the two t-shirts and pair of underwear that had fallen on top of a large, plastic black garbage bag. *I am glad everything didn't fall out*, he exclaimed in his head.

After gaining control of his bag and his footing, Henry quickly gathered in his culinary prizes. With three, four-day old ham sandwiches from the deli department, two oranges, and a partially moldy loaf of bread, he smiled at his bounty. He placed the food inside his shopping bag. With a massive grunt, he lifted himself over the top of the bin, keeping the shopping bag and its contents safe. Once out of the garbage bin, he grabbed his suitcase and searched for a comfortable spot to feast.

Henry kept walking and looking. Finally, he noticed a set of steps in back of the courthouse. Funny, he had never seen these before. The cement on the steps seemed to have mostly dried from the rainstorm. No one was there. Henry knew there was a chance he would be chased away, but he decided to go for it anyway.

He climbed to the third step and sat down. The cement was wetter than he thought. So, he grabbed his old blanket from the shopping bag and placed it underneath him. He sat down again. He looked over his bounty. Three sandwiches—that should last until tomorrow morning. Henry didn't think about whether the sandwiches were still safe to eat. He placed his suitcase on his lap and the shopping bag on top. With his left hand he reached in the bag to pull out his culinary prizes. "Let's see," he said aloud. "We have ham and cheese, ham and cheese, or ham and cheese." He laughed to himself. "I think I will choose ham and cheese." Thoroughly amused, Henry selected the sandwich that was on top, unwrapped the cellophane, and began to eat.

At first Henry ate quickly, devouring nearly half of the sandwich in a matter of seconds. Then, he slowed down. *Enjoy this*, he said to himself. *What am I in a hurry for?* To ensure that his pace of eating slowed, he placed the remaining part of the sandwich back into the top of the shopping bag.

He, then, reached into the bag in order to search for one of the two oranges. When he did this, he noticed something odd resting in between two of the T-shirts he retrieved after they had fallen out of the bag. He moved his left hand over the unidentifiable object. After a moment of uncertainty, he grabbed what felt like a ring. Old Man pulled out what seemed to be someone's wedding ring. The diamond was large, but he had no idea how much it was worth.

Henry studied the ring. *I wonder how it got here?* He stared at it with both disbelief and envy. He reminded himself that this could have been the ring he would have bought Ginny. His mind daydreamed for a bit. Then, he began to think about how to turn it in. The idea of keeping the ring was not an option.

Suddenly, Henry looked up. There in front of him was one of the three policemen who had approached the huddled group avoiding the rainstorm. The policeman noticed Henry before he saw the ring. It was instinct that drove the officer to the base of the cement courthouse steps. The officer saw the ring.

Henry started to stand up in order to give the policeman the ring. He began saying, "I just found…." However, before he could finish his sentence, the office told him to hand over the ring and put his hands on top of his head.

This time there would be no lawyer's fees. Henry had no money. The odds of probation without a lawyer seemed dim. "Counseling is out," he mumbled to himself.

Henry could not figure how the ring got there. "Could it have fallen off someone's finger when we were waiting during the rain?" His mind kept wondering.

Henry was driven to the police station and booked. He had no explanation, and the police did not want to hear one. After he was read his rights, he rested in a large holding cell with three other characters that made him seem civilized. He kept his distance from the others. After aimlessly wandering about the corner of his cell, he placed his back against the cement cell wall and slid to the floor. No one bothered him.

Henry's mind was a quagmire. In one way his future seemed more predictable now than it had three hours earlier. On the other hand, he longed for the uncertainty of the street. After battling his racing mind, he fell asleep.

He dreamed of Ginny. She looked just as she had when they first met. Henry really couldn't see himself, just her. Ginny looked beautiful. She wore a blue print Hawaiian dress that Henry had never seen before. Her eyes glowed as they stared into the mystical figure of Henry. The wedding ring floated from Henry's hand onto Ginny's finger. He heard the words,

"I do." All of the wedding guests, who were not clearly visible, began singing, "You are the sunshine of my life."

Henry looked at Ginny. She smiled. Ginny looked him in the eye and said, "Henry, I adore you." Henry's figure held her for a moment and said, "I love you from here to Mars." After all, that was their ritual.

Henry watched as the Ginny figure began to fade. Soon, only the ring was left. It was floating in the air. Unable to control the ring's path, it flew randomly in space. "Come back. Please, come back," Henry yelled. But neither Ginny nor the ring complied. The ring kept moving further and further away from Henry. Finally it appeared, rested on the third finger of the officer's left hand. "A perfect union," shouted the policeman.

Henry woke up. He looked around. One of his three roommates had disappeared. The other two continued to seem uninterested in an unkempt, homeless man.

Henry began to doze off again. He heard the noise of the door opening. A voice said, "You can go." Henry continued to sit. "You can go. You are cleared," said the voice.

Henry opened his eyes to see an officer standing in front of him. "We found the person who took that ring. We caught him with a lot of jewelry. When we asked him about the wedding ring, he admitted to taking that too. He said he dropped it in your shopping bag during that rainstorm." The officer waited. "Come on, get up. Unless you would rather stay here."

Henry never really thought about freedom before. Actually, he did when he flew his kite along the road filled with houses. That moment was the best way he could define freedom. Now, he even had a better definition. He heard the cell door close behind him. At the front of the police station, the officer wore latex gloves as he reunited Henry and his belongings. As Henry turned to go through the final door of the station, the officer said, "Sorry," as he took off his latex gloves.

Henry walked down the seven stairs that separated the precinct door from the street. He counted each step. He quietly whispered "one, two, three four, five, six, seven." By the time he got to seven, his voice could be heard down the block. The sun was shining. A dreary day had become quite promising.

Henry stopped at the garbage can to throw out his two remaining sandwiches. They didn't smell yet, but he didn't want to take a chance. *I'll keep the oranges*, he said to himself. *I think they are OK.*

· 16 ·

A New Love

As Old Man lay on the garage floor, he looked through the window and saw a distant rainbow. Not the most vivid rainbow. But a rainbow nonetheless! "Florence," he mumbled. Then, he smiled.

I was sitting on the bench right outside of that hardware store, remembered Old Man. His mind began to drift. The bench was a memorial to a man named Ebinezer Plotkin.

He wondered about whether Ebinezer Plotkin really deserved a bench. "Maybe he does," he mumbled.

As Old Man rested on the bench, he reached into a plastic garbage bag and pulled out cellophane containing two biscuits. He had picked the plastic bag out of the garbage can two blocks down. He couldn't believe that someone would throw away these two biscuits that were about to be his lunch. He had been without a place to live for a long time. Learning how to exist had not always been easy. In the beginning, he found it repulsive to take food out of a public garbage can. But he learned.

He opened the cellophane bag and grabbed one of the biscuits. He carefully replaced the twist tie on the bag in order to keep the second biscuit fresh for later. He was content. The day had not been particularly stressful. The weather was warm enough but the early morning rain had caused him to seek temporary shelter for a few moments at a time under the awnings in front of the shops on Main Street and on the side streets. No one had bothered him as he stood there for his allotted time. So Old Man was grateful. Now, as he sat on the bench, he looked up and saw a rainbow. He wanted to take this as a good sign- maybe a sign of luck.

He decided to take little bites of the biscuit. *It last longer that way.* Besides, the bench was comfortable. As he took his third little bite, he heard a woman's voice. "Aren't you going to share," the voice said.

Old Man was startled to see a rather attractive figure smiling at him. Her smile was appealing. She had all of her teeth, and they were not very yellow. She wore a soft-brimmed hat with a small feather off to the back. The woman sat down next to him on the bench. "Well, are you going to share or not?" She asked.

Old Man was a bit dumfounded. He had not been confronted like this before. His appearance had deteriorated, but his persona still had an indescribable appeal. He broke off a piece of the biscuit and handed it to her.

She asked, "Want some coffee?" Old Man nodded. "I'll be right back," she said. The woman got up. Old Man figured she was gone. But to his surprise, she returned a few minutes later with two paper cups filled with coffee. She asked, "Do you want the one with cream or not?"

"Not," he said. She handed him the cup of hot, black coffee in her left hand.

"That's good," she said, "because I like cream."

He thanked her. The two sat there saying nothing but they stared at the fading rainbow. After a couple of minutes, Old Man said, "I have another biscuit. Do you want some?"

Florence sat quietly and Old Man said nothing until she asked, "What is your name?"

"My name is Old Man," he answered.

"Old Man! You are too young to be an old man," she answered.

"Age has nothing to do with it. I feel like an old man and to me I look like an old man. So I call myself Old Man."

"Nice to meet you Old Man. I am Florence."

So, this how he met Florence! They did not say much to each other, but from the time they got up off Ebinezer's bench until that fateful day several weeks later the two were attached.

"Where do you live?" asked Florence that first day.

"Anywhere I can," he answered. "I tried shelters but they made me feel uncomfortable. It is colder on the street, but I am happier."

She asked, "Have you tried abandoned buildings?" Florence took Old Man's hand and the two of them walked. "Come with me. I will show you something," she said.

Florence led him through a series of side streets, past an abandoned warehouse. "Here. Here is where we can stay." She led him to the backside of the warehouse. The door was locked but the window next to it conveniently lifted up. "There are others here," she added. "But there is lots of room."

The first floor of the warehouse smelled dank. The cement floor was damp. There were several huge, very dusty cabinets spread throughout the first floor. As the two walked, their footsteps echoed.

"Come upstairs," said Florence. The two made their way up a circular metal staircase. Old Man grabbed onto the railing as he continued up. Florence was more confident. The second floor was divided into rooms. One room had a desk with no chair. Another room contained an old, dusty couch. The bathroom had a sink and toilet, but the water did not work.

Old Man did not know what to think. He was intrigued by Florence. He had been alone since he was forced out of the basement apartment with bars on the windows. That seemed like a long time ago. He had not minded being alone. He looked upon his isolation as penance for messing up his life. In many ways, he actually preferred street living to working.

Florence showed him to the third large room of the upstairs. "Here is where I stay. Gwen and Fred stay in the room over there. I met Gwen a while ago and she took me under her wing. And I don't know the names of the three who live in there."

Florence was a puzzler to him. She was put together better than almost any woman he had seen on the street. Her teeth were in good shape. She sounded smart. She was able to buy him a cup of coffee without having to beg. He did not know what to make of her. No matter what, he was grateful for the company. He missed Ginny. The idea of being with a woman excited him.

Florence set up the third room on the second floor as a little home for them to live in. That is what they did for nearly three months. Florence would show up with flowers. She would bring books back to the room. At night she would use a flashlight to read. Someone who had been living there before rigged up a chute off of the bathroom; the residents would urinate in the chute that would drop the liquid on the ground below. In general, life was good.

One day Florence went out on her own. She returned to the warehouse with paper and an inexpensive set of watercolor paints. Florence asked him, "What should I paint?"

Old Man wanted to ask her where she got the money to buy the paper and paints, but he decided to say nothing. "How about the place we met." So, he sat and watched Florence as she painted the bench with the two of them sitting on it. The painting was not perfect, but it was quite good. He knew she had taken lessons, perhaps years before.

Old Man finally asked Florence, "How do you have money to pay for paints and books?" He thought back on Ginny. He expected Florence to say that she stole them.

"I have a treasure hidden away. No one knows where it is but me. I can't even tell you. When I go there, I make sure no one is around. I take a few dollars at a time from the treasure. The money is mine. I did not take it."

Old Man never asked again. Florence would go off every two or three days for a couple of hours and return with some food and something for herself. One afternoon she returned with two large containers of chicken noodle soup and a porcelain doll. The doll was the size of her hand. She held it like a little girl would.

There was something about Florence that mystified Old Man. He was never frightened. *She does have these moments*, he thought.

Florence seemed perfectly normal almost all of the time. The two of them had interesting conversations once in a while. Mostly, though, they would sit next to each other and say very little. But there were moments when Florence would seem to drift off into another world. She was preoccupied. During these moments, she didn't hear anything Old Man said and paid no attention to him.

Then, about twelve weeks after they met, the two of them were sitting on that same bench. There was no rainbow. But the sweet smell of wisteria filled the sky. Old Man started to doze off when he heard Florence say, "Stay away from me." He quickly opened his eyes and looked around. There was no else there. Florence was turned away from him as if she was talking to a third person on the bench. But there was no one else. At first he thought Florence was dreaming but her eyes were wide open.

Florence again said, "Stay away from me." She sounded agitated. Old Man tapped her on the shoulder. She paid no attention. She repeated these same words over and over, at least ten times. Henry just sat there unsure what to do. Then, as if nothing had happened, Florence turned to Henry and smiled. She grabbed his hand, put her head on his shoulder and said nothing. This behavior never happened again.

A few days later, it was a warm September day when Florence and Old Man were walking near the large park. They could see the third hole of the golf course from where they were standing. He was telling Florence about how to make a "chip" shot. Suddenly, a booming voice shouted out. "We have been looking for you for months. And who is that man?"

Henry looked at Florence. Her spirits appeared broken. She grabbed Henry's hand. "Don't let them take me," she pleaded with Old Man. "Don't make them take me with them," she begged.

He was startled and instinctively held Florence. A young man who seemed to be in his thirties came to within a foot of him. "Let go of my mother," the son insisted. "Or I will call the police." He hesitated for a second and pointed his finger at Old Man. "I will have you arrested for kidnapping." Then, Florence's son made an error in judgment. He grabbed Old Man's hand and attempted to push him away.

Old Man knew the feeling. It was the same feeling Henry had decades ago with the bully. It was the same feeling he had in the bar with Arnie. Uncontrollably, Old Man summoned the spirit of the "The Rock" into his left fist. Without a warning, his left fist found that well right below the son's right eye and to the right of his nose.

Blood flowed. The son screamed. Florence remained calm. The police came.

Florence agreed to go with her son if he did not press charges against her companion. She agreed to return to the special home where she lived. Henry begged her not to go. "I have to," she answered. "Good bye. I love you."

And that was that. Florence was gone. Henry heard the son tell the policeman that his mother had walked away from the Nathanson Home several months ago. The family had hired a detective to locate her. However, the son had decided to bring his mother back on his own, rather than have the detective bring her. This was a decision that the son now had mixed feelings about.

Old Man continued to live at the warehouse for a few weeks. One day he returned there after some time at the fountain. He saw a construction crew starting the process of tearing the building down. Old Man asked one of the workmen if he could please go in and get his belongings. "I'm not supposed to, but I give you two minutes. Hurry up."

Old Man only wanted to grab two things. He grabbed the watercolor picture of the two of them on the bench and the ----porcelain doll. When he got to the street, he placed the picture that Florence had drawn and the doll in his shopping bag he had left with the workman. The picture and the doll remained with him for the rest of his life.

He had not thought of Florence in a long time. The doll was now safely placed at the bottom of the treasure chest next to the apartment building, but the watercolor was folded up neatly at the bottom of his shopping bag that rested next to his blanket on the cement floor of the garage.

· 17 ·

The Old Man's Lament

He debated which way to go. He knew he couldn't go back.

It was time for Old Man to wake up the girl. He looked at her. She slept so soundly. Her breathing was so deep. She had a contented smile.

He wanted to do something that would wake the girl up. He didn't want to touch her. He was afraid that would make the girl think something which wasn't true.

Suddenly, a feeling of loneliness took over Old Man's body. Once he left the girl, he would be alone again. Loneliness had rarely bothered him. During the past many years, he learned to live without much human contact. He did mumble to himself. But that was something he had always done, even in the prosperous years.

Over time, Old Man had witnessed what loneliness can do to people. He watched Henrietta, a veteran of the streets, carry on conversations with herself. He witnessed Abraham spending hours playing the harmonica he found outside of the high school. Abraham would introduce his harmonica as his best friend, Rhino. Then, he would play nonsensical songs that, to him, were symphonies.

Now, he thought about his own loneliness. He thought, "Who will bury me?"

His body shuddered. He rarely felt this vulnerable. His stomach felt hollow. All these years he was surviving, and his heart was so empty. *Who will bury me?*

His attention left the girl as his mind raced. His head pounded with that same question. *Who will bury me?*

He saw the image of Pauline. Pauline's body rested on the street curb. She might have been forty or she might have been eighty. After enough time on the street, life is ageless. He watched as the two officers called the ambulance that took Pauline away, never to be seen again. No one knew where she went, or where she was buried. *No one buried her*, thought Old Man.

"Pauline deserved better," he mumbled. Pauline never harmed anyone. She always had a smile. When Old Man first met Pauline, her teeth were just beginning to be covered with that grainy yellow tinge. By the time Pauline laid on the street corner, she had, perhaps, three or four teeth left. "But she had heart," he added to himself.

Pauline would say to him, "You don't belong here. You need to go back where you came from."

Henry would respond, "I wish I could."

"She deserved better," Old Man repeated. Then, he looked over at the girl.

Old Man reached into his shopping bag and took out the pen that he found lying on the sidewalk two days before. He tried to be quiet because he did not want the crumbling of the paper to be the noise that would awaken the girl. He looked back in the shopping bag, searching for a piece of paper. At the bottom, he found some old newspaper. "That won't do it," he said. Finally, he carefully tore a small piece from the top of the shopping bag.

Old Man began to write a poem to the girl.

> Roses are red.
> I like trees.
> If I die,
> Will you bury me?

He looked at the poem and, then, smiled. His loneliness was not gone, but he did feel better. He read the poem once more. Then, he decided to place the poem at the bottom of the shopping bag that now had a gash torn at its top. He knew it was time to go visit his friend at the grocery store.

He was ready to wake up the girl. *If there is a God*, he thought, *help me to do the right thing here*. He looked at the girl who started to move. Old Man was not religious. But, if religion mattered, this was the time. He watched her as a father would watch a daughter. He searched for the right words that would lead him down the right path. He struggled to come up with anything meaningful to say.

She stretched her arms and opened her eyes. She looked up at Old Man who was now sitting on top of the blanket that lay on the cement floor. In the daylight her eyes did not seem quite so deer like. They seemed even softer. She raised herself up on her left elbow and faced him. She looked at him in a kind way. She smiled. Old Man looked at her and smiled back. "Hello, father," she said. He did a double take.

Every moment of doubt that plagued Old Man these many years disappeared for an instant. Every second of self-deprecation that accompanied his thousands of nights sleeping on the streets vanished. Every hopeless moment that added up to thousands upon thousands of hopeless moments no longer haunted his mind.

Those simple words, "Hello, father," had pushed Old Man through the wall of fog that until a minute ago seemed impenetrable.

· 18 ·

The True Story

"I knew where to look for you," the girl said. "It didn't take long. Mom told me your name when I was fifteen. Before that she told me that she did not know your name. She said that she met you one night at a party and never saw you again. I believed her. It never seemed that she had ever lied to me before.

"I wrote your name with a felt tip pen on the neck of Sparky, my favorite stuffed animal. Every night I would hold Sparky and wonder what you were like. Mom said that she wasn't sure if you wanted to see me. She warned me that your life was different." The girl paused. "When she told me your name, she said that I should wait until I was a little older to find you. She said it might be difficult for me to accept you. I told her that I wanted to find you. So, she brought me to the fountain.

"There you were. Just sitting there. Mom said, 'He was a wonderful person. But things change.'"

Old Man just listened. He sat cross-legged on the blanket that rested on the cement basement floor. He felt ashamed. His heart ached. What had he become!

He remembered the day near the fountain when Ginny, with the baby carriage, had yelled to him. If he had stopped, he would have known. Maybe his life would have changed. Maybe not! But he knew that avoiding Ginny sealed his fate for a long time.

"So, I left the fountain without talking to you," she continued. I went home and cried. I cried for myself, and I cried for you. I wished that you were Sparky so I could hug you.

"I would go back to the fountain to look for you. Sometimes I would wait for hours. Sometimes you never came. Sometimes you would just walk by and not stop. Other times you would sit on the wall in front of the fountain. On the days when you sat on the wall, I would watch you. You seemed so kind. You smiled at those who passed you by. You did not look unhappy. I wanted to say 'hello,' but I couldn't."

Old Man smiled at the girl. She crawled over to him and gave him a hug. "I was afraid you would reject me," she whispered in his ear. "I was afraid you would tell me to go away."

Old Man hugged her back. He did not know how he would have behaved if the girl had reached out to him. He understood her worry. She may have been right.

The two remained in a heart-warming lock for minutes. Both had tears. They were tears of joy and tears of regret.

"I must smell terrible," he said.

The girl just moved her arms from Old Man's neck and grabbed both of his hands. She was surprised how rough his hand felt; they were like sandpaper. She said nothing about this.

"That was seven years ago when mom gave me your name. I still have Sparky. I kept going to the fountain looking for you. I guess I was afraid that one day you would stop showing up."

She cried again.

"But you kept coming back." She wiped the tears from her cheeks. Old Man squeezed her hands.

"Why…Why now," he said.

The girl smiled. "One day I was watching you at the fountain. As usual, you were sitting quietly. The snow was falling. You began to make a snowman. You were so wonderful with that little boy. The boy gave you his gloves. You knew they wouldn't fit, but you took them. Then, you and the boy used pennies for the eyes and took a carrot from someone to use as the nose." The girl paused. "The boy didn't care what you looked like or how you were dressed. He could see through. The boy could see your kindness. He could see that you could be trusted."

The girl looked at Old Man. Her eyes no longer looked both excited and hopeful. They transformed to the look of a warm, spring day. "At that moment, I knew I had to tell you. At that moment, I missed my father."

The girl again cried. So did Old Man. He tried to be funny. "If we don't stop crying, we are going to float away on this blanket." She laughed and wiped her cheek.

"What should I call you?" he asked.

"Molly or Mol," she replied. Then, she smiled again. "I will call you Father."

The two said nothing for a while. Finally, the girl continued. "At first, I was going to go to you at the fountain. But, I worried about telling you in front of other people. So, I made up a plan. I would follow you and pretend that I was in trouble."

The girl told her father that pretending was easy to her since she had been acting parts since she was a little girl. Her mother had joined a community theater and brought her daughter to rehearsals. One time, when the girl was five, the director asked Molly if she would stand in for the part of a young daughter in the play; the little girl who was selected for the part was sick. It took one rehearsal, and Molly became the young daughter.

"From there, I kept doing parts. I did love it. I learned to use my imagination when I played different parts. That's what I did last night. I imagined finding you. I did not want to tell you right out that I was your daughter. I was worried that you would run away. So, I imagined how to get you to follow me here. I wasn't sure if it would work, but it did." Molly paused. "And here we are."

The girl looked sorrowfully at him. "I am sorry I lied to you. Yesterday, I thought of it as playing a part in a play. Today, I see that I lied." She gave him a quick hug and, then, moved back. "I promise I will not lie to you again."

Old Man looked at her. She was even prettier than he originally thought. What had he done to deserve a child like this? What would he do now? He wondered where she lived. He didn't want to ask too many questions.

"How do you feel?" asked Molly.

"I am happy and confused," he responded. "My heart is full of happiness. But my mind is confused." He thought for a moment. He decided to ask one question. "Where is your mother?"

"I will tell you about it later. Trust me on this."

"Are you sure I am your father?"

"I asked my mother over and over if the man at the fountain was really my father. Then, five years ago when I needed a passport to study in England, she showed me my birth certificate. It says Ginny Forsythe is my mother and Henry Patrick is my father."

"That's me." He began to cry again. "I wish I had known."

Molly grabbed his hands gently. "We can't change what has happened. But we can look to the future."

The last time he heard those words was the day Ginny returned from her first trip to the police station. She said, "Henry, I love you. I am sorry. We can't change what has happened. But we can look to the future." Henry was sure that his daughter learned those words from her mother.

Molly got up. She pulled on her father's hands, motioning him to get up also. With some difficulty, he complied. "Let's go home," she said.

Henry looked at her quizzically. "Where is home?"

"Here," Molly answered. "This is home. This is my home. Now, this is your home."

"I don't understand."

"This is the house I was brought up in. We are in my garage. I am sorry that I didn't tell you right away. But I was worried that you would get frightened and run away. I needed to make sure that you would not be afraid.

"So, I created a play. A girl is upset. She is depressed. She is helpless. I played upon your kindness to get you to come here." The two were still standing by the blankets in the garage. "I am sorry that I misled you. But I didn't know any other way."

Henry didn't say anything. He understood. He was grateful that she cared that much to go to such trouble. He asked, "Is your mother in the house?" Henry was hoping that Ginny was part of this entire plot. The idea of a real family now excited him.

"Mom is not here," Ginny said. "She is in hospice. She has breast cancer and is going to die soon. She is on some heavy drugs. Sometimes she is aware that I am there and sometimes doesn't know. It has been a difficult year.

Henry was heartbroken.

"Come, let's go home," Molly said. She led her father through the garage door, across the yard and into the bungalow.

· 19 ·

Ginny's Fate

Ginny was pregnant. But she never told Henry. She left when the tensions between them got too unbearable. She knew it was her fault. She couldn't see a way to restore peace.

So, after the second court appearance and a promise of more counseling with restitution and warning from the judge that prison was next, Ginny left Henry. She had skills. She had been to college. However, she did have a criminal record that would not be expunged for many years. Nevertheless, her most important asset was her charm. She knew that her survival depended upon her charm. She would have to charm her way to survival. The how and where were unknown.

Henry had stayed away for her exit. He was too emotional. He loved Ginny more than he imagined he ever could love anyone. He believed she loved him with as much emotion. So her exit was just too painful.

It didn't take Ginny long to pack her one large suitcase, which she had not stolen, with clothes and one other large valise, which she did steal, with her computer and other paraphernalia.

Ginny was not frightened. She didn't seem to know the true meaning of fear. She was concerned, but not afraid. She lingered for a moment at the door to their apartment. Never one to cry, she shed a couple of tears and, unceremoniously, made her way to the elevator and out the apartment building front door.

Ginny was not a real planner but she had made a plan. With very little money that she saved from her job, she knew that she had to be dependent on someone. Ginny hated to be dependent on anyone. But survival is survival.

So, she had contacted her first cousin Sarah. Sarah and Ginny had been like sisters for a few years while in elementary school. The two grew apart as they moved through their late teens, even though they both lived in the same town. Now Ginny needed Sarah. Sarah reached out, although Sarah's husband was not too excited about the arrangement.

From the moment Ginny arrived at Sarah's house, there was tension that Ginny worked hard to lessen. First, Ginny had not told Sarah that she was pregnant. Second, Ginny's husband had underestimated how attractive the new guest would be and seemed to have been aroused from the moment Ginny entered the front door.

Ginny sensed trouble. But she had no other choice. She would make this work. She would help around the house. She would stay away from Sarah's husband. She would get a better job somewhere, even though she would have a child in a little less than seven months. And she would leave this house to raise her child in peace. And, if her prayers were answered, she would ask Henry to forgive her.

Life doesn't always work the way we plan. Ginny's plan, as it turned out, had some holes in it. The largest one was Sarah's husband who kept touching Ginny every time he could when his wife was absent. The husband knew that the guest was vulnerable, even though he didn't immediately know that she was with child.

Ginny watched Sarah and her husband talk and act. They did not seem to have an ideal life together. He was cruel. Sarah did not seem happy.

Ginny wanted to tell her cousin about the husband's predatory behavior. She just couldn't. Who was Ginny to show up and complain about one of her hosts? It would only be logical that Ginny would be perceived as the real predator. Ginny knew this would result in her being on the street. She kept her mouth shut and continued to try and stay, at least, two arm's lengths away from him.

This did not always work. The touches became increasingly intrusive. It was almost as if the husband believed he had the right to be intimate with the guest because she, after all, was living there for free. Finally, one day after about five weeks at the house, Ginny was setting the table for dinner. The husband sneaked up behind his guest and placed his hands on her breasts. Ginny jumped away and screamed. "Don't ever do that again."

"Or what?" he said. "Or you will leave? I don't think so."

"I am pregnant," she screamed.

"You think I am stupid. That makes it perfect," Sarah's husband responded. "You can't get pregnant twice."

Ginny darted out of the dining room, shedding several more tears than the day she left Henry. As she moved through the kitchen, she saw Sarah next to the swinging door that separated the two rooms. Sarah's eyes were filled with even more tears.

Ginny stopped. "I am sorry," she said. "I didn't..." And she couldn't say anymore.

Her cousin shook her head. "It's not you. It's him." Sarah paused. Ginny just stood in front of her. Sarah's tears stopped and her posture suddenly showed a confidence. "Help me," she said. "Help me to get him out of here. Help me to leave him. Help me to start a better life."

Ginny gave Sarah a hug. Both were crying as they held onto each other.

Ginny told Sarah that she needed a plan. She had to do things strategically. This approach was uncharacteristic of Ginny.

Ginny and Sarah agreed it was time to act. The first step was to make Ginny less vulnerable. She had been sleeping in the spare bedroom upstairs next door to Sarah and her husband. Sarah moved into the spare bedroom with Ginny. Her husband got the message.

The second step was to get a good attorney.

The two of them searched for the name of the best divorce lawyer they could find. When they called the lawyer's assistant, she told them that her boss required a retainer of $4,000. As a result, they located the second-best divorce attorney who worked out quite well.

The husband, surprisingly, only threw one tantrum. This did not happen when Sarah told him about seeing the lawyer and filing for divorce. At that moment he laughed at her as if to say, "You don't have the balls."

The tantrum occurred when the sheriff showed up with a court order demanding that he leave and not go within five hundred feet of his wife. The husband yelled and screamed. The sheriff escorted him out the front door. With the exception of a predetermined day for the husband to retrieve his belongings, under supervision, he never returned and never bothered Sarah again. "Good riddance, bitch," he yelled up the stairs on his way out, even though she was not present.

To make things simple, Sarah took the house in the divorce settlement. "Will you stay?" she asked Ginny. "Stay for a while. I will be lonely. You can raise the baby here until you want to leave."

So it was. The two young attractive ladies shared the house. Ginny raised her baby daughter there, and Sarah became a second mother. The two women, each, had periodic relationships with men and, occasionally, brought home a male companion, but for the most part they were content to be with each other.

Ginny found a job as a secretary with a furniture company. Molly did not know of her mother's shoplifting. Because of her record, Ginny's job opportunities were limited. After being at the furniture company for two years, her bosses encouraged her to move to the sales floor. The rest is history. She became the top salesperson, earning more money than she had imagined possible. As for Sarah, after a couple of years, she met an attorney and eventually married him. "He is a really nice guy," Molly reported. When Sarah left to move in with her new husband, she sold Ginny the house at a discount price.

· 20 ·

The Decisive Blow

"What did you mother say about me?" asked the Henry.

Molly looked a little surprised. She never expected her father to ask that question. It was almost as if he suspected that Ginny might have badmouthed the father of her child. Molly did not respond right away. She thought for a moment. Her mother had said quite a bit about her father once the two of them had seen Henry at the fountain. Molly remembered. She asked her mother, "How did he get that way?"

Ginny just answered, "Things happen. Sometimes they are for the better and sometimes for the worse." Then, Ginny added to her daughter, "This seems like worse, but you never know."

Molly smiled. "She always said good things about you."

"Tell me something she said. I don't have to know, but I want to know," he added.

"Mom said you were unafraid to do what was right. She said that was one of the things that made you special." Molly was telling the truth. Ginny told her daughter the truth.

"Mom said that one time the two of you were walking in the forest on your way to a picnic."

Henry instantly knew what his daughter was talking about. He had not thought of this for a long, long time.

Henry and Ginny had lived together for nearly six months. "Let's have a picnic," said Ginny. It was a glorious summer day. There was a soft wind and the oddest shaped clouds covered the warm sky. Ginny loved to lie on her back and tell Henry what the shapes of the clouds reminded her of. She would say, "Give me a category." At first, Henry had no idea what she meant.

"A category is a category," responded Ginny. "It's stuff that goes together, like kinds of vegetables."

On this particular day, Henry gave Ginny the category of Shakespeare's Tragedies. He would sometimes say a category that he was sure Ginny did not know. On this day, he was shocked to realize that his love remembered all those Shakespearean tragedies that she read in high school and college.

The two of them walked further into the state forest with their picnic lunches and a large blanket. They began walking down a dirt trail that led to another steep dirt trail that led to a small, but enticing waterfall. Ginny carried the picnic basket, and Henry cradled the large blanket. There was a rock at the top of the waterfall where the two had picnicked the summer before.

As they walked down the first dirt trail, there was a clearing, a small meadow filled with balding grass. Ginny lay down on the greenest piece of grass and looked up at the Cirrus clouds above; they were mixed into the blue sky. "That cloud over there looks like Romeo. Do you see the head at the top? Next to the head is a cup. That's the cup filled with poison."

Henry was about to say, "I am impressed," when he looked over past the clearing into a section of the woods away from the dirt path. He saw a rather large man slapping a rather tiny woman. He could not hear the contact, but Henry was sure about what he saw. Ginny continued to match the next cloud to another Shakespearean character. She was oblivious to what Henry saw.

"I can't believe it," said Henry.

"I knew you would be impressed," she answered.

"No, over there," Ginny sat up and witnessed the second slap followed by a punch.

Without hesitation, Henry ran over to the large man and the tiny woman. "Stop it," he yelled. "What do you think you are doing?"

The large man turned to Henry who was now only a few feet away. "Mind you own business," threatened the stranger.

Henry looked at the tiny girl who couldn't have been out of her teens. The stranger took two steps towards Henry and gave him a push, much like the man at the coffee house. Henry immediately connected the stranger to his inner emotions. He felt the surge that had saved him as a child and had gotten him into so much trouble as an adult.

Henry's body filled with that volcanic energy he had harnessed as a youth. His heart raced as he summoned "The Rock." The stranger had just finished the second push when Henry unloaded his infamous left hand into the well right below the stranger's right eye. The first time Henry had ever thrown this punch, he was not quite sure if it worked. This time Henry knew that the punch connected. The big stranger fell backwards. The momentum of his body was beyond his control. The back of his head smashed against the rock.

Henry did not wait to see if the stranger was still alive. He went over to the tiny girl. "Let's go," he ordered. By now Ginny was close by. She had abandoned the picnic basket and the blanket.

At first the tiny girl did not move. "Let's go," Henry yelled this time. The girl rose to her feet.

"Come over here," said Ginny. "Come with me."

Henry followed. He quickly diverted to the picnic basket and blanket. He picked them both up and stayed behind the two women as they escaped the dirt path and entered the parking lot. Henry kept looking behind him, making sure the large man had not gained coherency.

"Mom told me that story a few times," said Molly. "She was very proud of you." Molly's eyes briefly looked up at the ceiling of the kitchen. "She never told me the rest of the story."

Old Man shook his head. "It got a bit strange. Your mother probably didn't want to scare you."

Molly wasn't sure what to say. She finally settled on, "So what happened?"

"We ran to the parking lot. Your mother and the young girl were in front. I kept looking behind me to make sure that the guy didn't come after us. He never appeared. We ran to the car. At first, the young girl didn't want to get in, but your mom convinced her that she had to get away from that man."

As Henry, Ginny, and the young girl left the parking lot of the forest, each of them was fixated on the end of the path that led to the asphalt. The girl propped herself on her knees in the back seat to get a good view; Ginny, in the front seat, turned from side to side; Henry kept glancing into the side mirror and then, into the rear-view mirror as he backed out from his parking space and moved towards the exit.

About fifty yards down at the exit of the lot was a park ranger in a booth. This was the moment of truth for the three of them. Do they tell the ranger what happened or do they just leave?

The girl noticed the ranger standing in the booth ahead. "Please, please don't say anything," she begged. "Please, my life depends on it."

As the car moved to within a few yards of the ranger booth, Henry yelled to the young girl, "Sit in your seat and put your seat belt on." The girl complied and Henry waved at the ranger in the booth. The ranger waved back.

The girl was relieved. Henry drove out of the state forest down the highway for several miles. He was confident that the man had not followed them. He was worried that the large man had died when he hit his head on the rock.

Ahead on the right was an A & W Root Beer stand. Henry pulled the car in the parking place right in front of the entrance. He turned to the young girl. "Hungry?"

With their sandwiches and French fries in front of them, the three, at first, sat silently. Then, Henry turned to the girl. He started to say, "Do you want to tell me what was going on back there?" But he changed his mind after the words "Do you...." He instead phrased the question, "What was going on back there?" He needed to know and did not want the girl to say, "NO."

The young girl did not say anything. She looked at her hamburger and not up at Henry. "We put ourselves on the line for you. You have an obligation to tell us what was going on," Henry said to her.

Henry looked at Molly.

"So, did she tell you?" asked Molly.

Henry nodded. "It took a while but we found out that she was a runaway who became a prostitute. She was only seventeen."

"Who was the guy?" asked Molly.

Henry shook his head. "The guy was her pimp. The girl had decided to create a little side business. She would give the pimp most of her money but kept a little on the side for herself."

Molly looked intrigued. "So the guy found out."

Henry shook his head again. "He probably would have broken her nose and who knows what else. She was beat up pretty bad when we found her. If that ranger had looked closely, he never would have let us out of the state park."

"So what happened?"

"You mom and I brought her home with us. You should have seen the stares from Mr. and Mrs. Arnold, the people who lived in the apartment next door. They happened to be coming out when we were coming in." Henry reminisced for a minute. Molly did not say anything.

"She ran away from her home a year before. Your mom was even more upset than I was. The girl stayed with us for a few days. Each day one of us would stay home with her because we knew that she would leave if someone weren't there to encourage her to stay. By, maybe, the fifth day she said she wanted to go home. We had been suggesting this. Your mom was great at encouraging her but not coming on too strong."

"So did she go home?" Molly asked.

"The next day your mom and I both took off from work. My boss was getting angry that I had missed three days in a week, but I told him it was a family emergency. At that time, your mom worked for Family Services; so she could explain the time. Anyway, we bought her a new dress and drove her five hours south to a little town called Ellsworth. We had called her mother two days before when we found out where she was from."

"What did her mother say?"

"Her mother cried. She wanted to come get her. We convinced her that it was better if we brought her home." Henry paused. "Of course, we knew the risk. She could sneak out of the apartment, and we would be in trouble. We were supposed to call the police, but we knew that the girl would be frightened at the idea of having to face that big guy again in court."

"But you knew you had to get her out of that bad situation," said Molly.

"Right. Your mom was a great judge of character most of the time. She told me on the second day with the young girl in our apartment that the girl wanted to go home. So, we brought her home."

"What happened?"

"It all worked out. The mother cried. The girl cried. Your mother cried. I cried. We all had a chicken dinner, and your mom and I left."

Molly asked, "Did you ever find out what happened to the guy?"

Henry shook his head. He was used to stroking his scraggly beard in moments like this. But he had shaved it off during his first hour in the house; it took three disposable razors that Molly had in the bottom drawer of the vanity. As he was cutting the mass of hairs on his face, he considered keeping a tamed version of the beard. Then, he realized that every time he looked in the mirror he would not see a neatly trimmed beard but the unkempt one he was cutting. He vowed to be clean-shaven for the rest of his life, however long that might be. So, he stroked his chin.

"The guy, the guy," responded Henry. "We did hear from the guy." He paused to reflect. "I wasn't sure what happened to him. I figured he didn't die because we never heard from the police. If he had died, the police would have interviewed the owners of every car in the parking lot at the state forest. I am sure there was some kind of a camera there."

"So, what happened?" Molly asked. She was on the edge of her chair.

"Well, about a week after bringing the girl, her name was JoAnne, back to her home, your mother and I were walking down Bing's Alley Way. We were going to get some dinner at the deli there. Your mother always loved their chicken soup."

"I remember. As a kid she would take me there all the time. I would have the potato pancakes with apple sauce." Molly realized that she had digressed. "Anyway…"

"Anyway, we were walking to the deli sometime around sunset. There was no one around us. We heard a voice. The voice said, 'Remember me?' We both turned around and saw the big guy from the woods. Your mom and I were frightened. I hadn't thought of this guy since we dropped off JoAnne. Now, here he was."

"What did he do?"

"He made a mistake. I think he intended to kill us. I am not sure. No one was right around us because we had taken the alleyway as a shortcut. We both had the same idea – to run. Now, all of this happened in a matter of a few seconds. The guy talked; we were surprised to see him; we turned to run. But the guy grabbed you mother's arm. This was his mistake."

"Why?"

"Your mother always carried a can of mace with her. She had been robbed before I met her. She told me, 'I will never let that happen again.' She spent time practicing. She practiced unzipping her purse and taking out the can of mace."

"So, she maced him?"

"She had practiced for this very situation. With one hand she unzipped her purse. The big guy pulled her in to him. I initially took a few steps away from the guy. But when he reached out and grabbed your mom's arm, I moved closer to him. As the guy was pulling your mom in, she grabbed the can of mace and sprayed him in the face."

"Did you run then?"

Henry sort of smiled. "We should have run. I was coming towards the guy. I could see your mom spraying the mace. I could see the guy grabbing for his eyes. I guess it was instinct. I reached back with my left hand and punched him the same way I had in the woods."

"Then, did you run then?"

"I just stood there. For an instant, I didn't even pay any attention to your mom. I grabbed his ankles and lifted them into the air. I watched him fall backwards. As he fell, he hit his head on the sharp edge of a metal garbage bin. His body stopped moving. He didn't fall to the ground. His feet were on the ground, but his head rested on the sharp edge of the bin."

"Was he dead?

"I decided we needed to get the police for this one. So, your mom ran to the street to find a cop. I waited with the body. I was hoping he wouldn't suddenly wake up and attack me. But he just lay there."

"Was he dead?"

"Yes. The police came. We told them that this man tried to rob us. We did not mention the part with JoAnne. She needed peace. We were on the evening news and everything."

Molly looked surprised. "I can't believe mom never told me the second part of the story."

"I think it was an event she would like to forget," responded her father.

"Did you ever hear from JoAnne again?"

"No and that was OK."

· 21 ·

His True Friend

Henry had wondered about Ginny since Molly had told him the truth. It only had been a couple of days since he had slept on the garage floor. The softness of a comfortable mattress had hypnotized his thinking. Now after a couple of warm, cozy nights of real sleep, his mind focused only on Ginny.

On the first night in the house, Molly said to him, "I want you to sleep in mom's room," Molly said.

Henry, at first, fought the idea. "I don't think that's a good idea."

"Mom definitely would want you there," Molly answered. "No arguments."

When he first climbed into bed, Henry could detect Ginny's scent. *I probably am imagining it*, he thought. *But it doesn't make any difference if I am making it up or not*, he mused to himself.

Then, he was so exhausted that his thought of his love faded. He only centered on sleep which he did for twelve hours that first night.

Now, he had been in his new home for two nights. He needed to know more about Ginny.

Henry couldn't imagine what she was like now. Ginny had always been so vibrant, so alive. Maybe, in spite of her pain, she still had that spirit. The reality of Ginny suffering could be more painful than he wanted to bear. The idea of looking at her smile and realizing that she would soon die, frightened him.

Henry recognized that he was being selfish. He and Ginny had spent only a short time together. Poor Molly, she had lived her whole life with her mother.

Henry walked from his room into the kitchen. On the counter he found a note.

"I had to go to work. We are shooting a commercial. I won't be home until 7:00 or 8:00. Food in refrigerator. Love you."

He smiled. His daughter was a star. Even though she made her living doing commercials, voiceovers and some theatre, to him she was a star.

He wondered what he would do for the day. He thought about the idea of returning to the streets clean-shaven with his clean hair, with his clean body, with his clean clothes. But he rejected this idea. It would be like taunting those who were not as fortunate as he. *I am sure they will have no idea who I am,"* he thought. *But still it is wrong.*

So, Henry spent the day writing poetry. He wrote a poem to Molly, a poem to Ginny, and a poem to Freddie Martin whose death still haunted him. The final two lines of Freddie Martin's poem stayed with him for the rest of the day.

> My soul is haunted by what I should have done
> My behavior made your tragic ending forgone.

146

He had seen so many people whose tragic endings seemed to be forgone. But Freddie's did not have to be that way, he thought. At that moment he was tempted to go out and buy a pint of Jack Daniels, but he pushed the idea from his mind. *No more Jack Daniels and no more creamed spinach!*

Instead his head floated. From Freddie Martin, his images changed to another Freddie – Crazy Freddie. Everyone called him Crazy Freddie. No matter the weather, he would stand in front of the old bank building on Main Street, in a T-shirt and wave to everyone walking by. He would do this every day, seven days a week between 1:00 and 3:00 p.m. Police, social services, and every other form of government employee took turns trying to get him to stop. However, these do-gooders faced one major obstacle – the public.

Soon after Crazy Freddie began his ritual, a reporter for the Post wrote a story about this man's odd behavior. It turned out that Crazy Freddie was a war hero from Vietnam. It turned out that he was not really that crazy. When interviewed he was actually very coherent. "After I got home from Vietnam and people spit on me for doing what I thought was right, I decided that this world is both worthless and absurd." This is what Freddie told the reporter.

Several times these government agencies tried to take Freddie away to a shelter, but he just returned to the same area. Every day he would appear in front of the bank and greet the people.

At first, the officials of the bank were mortified. It was the second week of Freddie's ritual when the officials called the police to remove Freddie. Before the police could make him disappear, the inevitable confrontation had drawn a rather large crowd. The large crowd began demanding that the officers leave Freddie alone. Soon local news stations were running stories about Freddie.

"We have a public relations nightmare," blurted Hayston Jennings, the chairman of the bank, two days after the confrontation and one day after the newspaper article. "People are already pulling their money out. The guy's a friggin' war hero."

"What should we do?" asked Jennings of the bank's chairman.

"Let him be. If he wants to greet customers wearing a T-shirt in the middle of winter, let him," replied the chairman.

Of course, the bank officials worried that every unusual behavior from every strange character in the area would soon be exhibited on the lawn in front of their bank. But this was not the case. Crazy Freddie, who was not very crazy, had the venue all to himself.

Henry smiled when the image of Freddie appeared in his mind. Too bad he died, he thought. Henry had walked to the town green cemetery to witness Freddie's funeral a few years ago. Even the mayor was there.

Henry thought how much he loved Freddie. Freddie was the only one he knew during this phase of his life who was totally coherent. This was the irony; the person whom everyone thought was crazy was actually saner than most people around him. The two of them would spend hours talking about the world. On days when they could grab a discarded newspaper from the trash, the two would read it together and comment about world events. Freddie was the only one with whom Old Man divulged his real name.

Because of Freddie's fame, he always received food and money that he shared with Henry. "You are my best friend. Really, you are my only friend," Freddie confided. "Hank," this is what Freddie called him, "you and I are different. You are still searching. I have given up. There is nothing for me to find. I am happy in the absurdity of my life. But I worry about you. You are going to need more. I am no longer religious. But you are my one prayer if there is a God of justice. I hope you find somebody to take you out of this."

When Freddie finished his words, Henry felt warm inside. He loved Freddie. He knew that somewhere Freddie was smiling. He could hear his friend say, "I am happy for you."

After Freddie's burial, the bank chairman, realizing an economic bonanza, set up "The Freddie Scholarship Fund for Returning Vets." Henry shook his head as he thought of the big poster with Freddie's picture in front of the bank. Above the photo were the words:

> Set up a Freddie account with $1000 or more and we will help a Veteran pay for school.

Henry remembered the first time he saw the poster. He stood in front of the bank and yelled out, "Freddie you have brought absurdity to a new level. God, I love you."

· 22 ·

The Moment of Truth

"I want to go see your mother," said Henry.

"I was hoping you would say that," said Molly. "The place mom is in is the nicest one I could afford. Fortunately, mom had taken out special insurance several years ago that would go towards something like this. The insurance will run out in a year or so. I know she will not make it that long,"

"We will have to figure something out," he responded.

Henry wasn't sure if he really wanted to see Ginny. He was afraid. He was worried that his memory of Ginny would become victimized by a terrible reality. But his heart begged him to go. "Yes, I am sure I want to go," he blurted out.

"I stopped to see mom on my way home. She is pretty drugged up. So don't be alarmed. Sometimes when I am there, she doesn't open her eyes. Yesterday she was more alert. But I didn't tell her about you."

"What did you talk about?"

"She asked how Sarah was doing. I told her Sarah's daughter had just had a baby and that Sarah wanted to come next week. This made her so happy. Sometimes, I am never sure what to say. I want her to hear happy thoughts. It's just sometimes the world seems so awful. I asked the doctor what to do. She said to make a list of three or four positive ideas or events to bring up." Molly began to cry. Her father came over and hugged her. "We can go tomorrow morning. She is better in the morning."

Henry smiled. Underneath his smile was the fear of the unknown. He had faced it every day on the streets. But this feeling was different. On the streets, he worried about his physical wellbeing. Now his fear was about his emotional wellbeing.

After a simple dinner of grilled chicken and asparagus, he gave Molly a kiss on her cheek and told her, "I am tired. I love you. Thank you for everything."

Molly knew that her father was troubled about the visit. She understood his anxiety and wished she could say something to make him feel better. But words escaped her. So she smiled back and gave him a kiss on the cheek. "Good night," she said. "Sleep well." She watched him as he made his way down the hallway.

He stared at the ceiling as he lay in bed. There was no sense in trying to get to sleep. He couldn't. His mind was racing. The thoughts were all incomprehensible. There were no clear images. There was only chaos that seemed to be pulled by an enormous gravitational force of uncertainty.

Time was not relevant. It didn't matter if the time was midnight or 2:00 a.m. His mind kept racing. Then, as if a gigantic puppet master pulled a string, he was asleep.

Even sleep was chaotic. He dreamed of Ginny spinning. Her image moved with increasing speed only to slow down to a standstill. This progression occurred over and over, until finally, she was sucked into some kind of black hole that devoured her. In the dream, Henry watched. It was as if he were on the other side of a tipping point. He remained motionless as his beloved Ginny spun and then stopped. She said nothing. At one point, Ginny reached for him. He was unclear if she was asking for help or encouraging him to join her. He was unable to do either. It was as if he became a fixed point in the galaxy.

Henry watched without expression as Ginny's voluptuous figure became stretched into an elongated noodle while she was sucked into oblivion.

Henry could see himself. When Ginny was no more, he turned away from the gravitational force. "I will be there soon," he heard himself say. "I will be soon."

His image grew and multiplied until there were countless representations of him. They were lined up single file and appeared to go on forever. Again he heard himself. "Which one is real? Which one is real?"

He heard Ginny's voice. It was a soft, reassuring voice. "There is no reality. There only is what you think is reality."

Then, Henry woke up. He glanced at the clock. It was 5:30. He remembered his dream. He wanted to find its meaning. But he had no idea where to start. "I wish I could figure it out," he mumbled. Then, he lay back down and stared at the ceiling.

He thought of Ginny on the bed next to him. He fantasized that the two of them were making love. He knew that his fantasy rested on an unrealistic hope. He knew that his reality would not permit him to believe that the facts of the present could be changed with the wave of a magic wand.

Molly and her father walked to the Fairview Hospice complex. As they walked up the path towards the main entrance, Henry felt a surge of anger. *Why had this happened to Ginny? After all, she isn't that old.* It was ironic to him that he had spent so many cold nights alone on the street, so much time in unfriendly environments, and yet, his memory of her was perfectly intact. He wished he could trade places.

"Mom's room is over here," said Molly pointing to the hallway on the right. "Remember what I told you." Her father nodded.

Molly had told him not to expect too much. "You have to remain calm, even if she is not alert. She may not remember you at first and only see you as someone who has come to spend time with her. Just smile at her and she will know who you are. You are going to feel lots of emotions. Don't let them make you negative in any way. I have been through the whole range of emotions."

The two of them knocked on Ginny's door. Ginny still looked beautiful to Henry. She was barely awake when they entered. But a warm smile showed when she saw Molly. Henry immediately wanted to cry but managed to stifle his tears. Molly looked over and could see the emotional swell around her father's eyes. "Hi mom," Molly said.

Ginny looked at Molly and then at Henry. It was a look of curiosity seeming to ask: Who is this? Ginny's eyes had a curiosity that seemed to indicate some recognition of the unknown visitor, even though she couldn't quite make an identification. Molly smiled at her mother reassuringly. The one thing she had learned was to make her mom feel comfortable, not to frighten her in any way.

Henry stood next to Molly and said nothing. He tried to smile but it was difficult. He tried to look relaxed, not tense, but his body experienced an unwelcomed stress.

Ginny suddenly shouted, "Henry?" Ginny looked at him. Henry could see a tear come from each of her eyes.

"How much you have missed?" said Ginny. "Isn't our daughter beautiful?"

Henry just smiled. He wasn't sure what to say. "She is as beautiful as you," answered Henry.

At that moment a young female helper from the facility came into the room. Henry was unsure what her title was. She gave Ginny two pills and waited until Ginny swallowed.

Molly introduced Henry to the worker. "This is my father," she said. The helper seemed surprised because Henry had been absent from her patient's life.

"She is so nice," Ginny said about the young lady. "She has a smile on her face. I love to see smiles, don't you?"

Henry saw this as a chance to, at least, say something. "I love smiles, too," he said.

Molly gave her mother a big hug and said," I will leave you two alone for a while." Then, Molly gave her father a hug and went out of the room.

Henry sat down on the edge of the bed. "I am so sorry."

"For what?" said Ginny.

"That day when you saw me at the fountain. I ran away. You ran after me. But I kept running. If I had only waited, if I had only stopped, our lives could have been so different."

Ginny only looked. "You are here now," she said. "That's what matters."

Ginny tried to pull her body up against the bed's headboard. Henry reached over and gently lifted her so that her head was raised against the pillow.

Henry wanted to again start crying when he realized that her body was so emaciated.

Ginny spoke. "I would watch you at the fountain. Your eyes always showed your kindness."

Henry did start to cry. "I have always loved you." He moved his head to hers and gave his only true love a soft, quick kiss on the lips.

Henry remembered the roses he brought with him. He had put them on the bureau when he came into the room. He stood up from the edge of the bed and went to the bureau. He picked up the roses and brought them to Ginny.

He took one rose from the bunch and handed it to Ginny. She smiled and tried to smell it. He put the rest of the flowers down on the table next to the bed. "You are the sunshine of my life," he said.

"I love you from here to Mars," Ginny said.

The tears filled their four eyes. "Come lay next to me," she said.

That is how the two spent the rest of the afternoon, saying very little, just laying next to each other on the bed.

Henry went to see Ginny every day until she died ten days later. Henry was with her the moments leading up to her passing. He and Molly crawled into bed with Ginny during her final moments. They held Ginny until several minutes after her final breath.

Seconds before she died, Ginny managed to say in a faint voice, "Molly I love you. Henry, I love you from here to Mars."

Fighting back tears, Henry said, "You are the sunshine of my life." Those were the final words that Ginny heard.

• 23 •

Old Man Becomes a Father

Henry sat quietly in the bedroom of his new house. He never imagined that he would ever have a home. His heart was light, almost giddy. Then, he felt guilty. He had done nothing to buy this house. He had done nothing to provide for his child. Instead, his child provided for him. It was not supposed to be this way.

He wondered if the guilt would go away. Could he live with the idea that he was saved by his daughter and not the other way around? The guilt was like a ghost whose reflection haunted him.

Yet, in spite of this sudden explosion of self-pity, Henry knew he could not leave. He was not about to abandon this girl who so cleverly had captured him. No, he knew that he must live with the guilt. He must hope that he could do something that would balance the inequality that now existed.

After all those years on the street, after all the evenings alone, he lived in a dream world. His bedroom was an illusion that became a reality when he looked out of the window. There was a rainbow. It was a signal – perhaps from Ginny or perhaps from Florence or perhaps from someone he never knew.

Henry again thought of Ginny. How he wished things had been different. *Maybe this is all part of the plan*, he thought to himself. *Maybe I have reached here for a reason.*

Henry had always thought of Ginny every day, even when he spent those weeks with Florence. Ginny was the love of his life. Now, waking up and going to bed would constantly rekindle thoughts of the woman he never stopped missing.

Henry looked at himself in the mirror. His hair was cut. His hands were clean. His beard was gone. He realized that all those years had aged him, but he did not look too bad. He looked presentable. He looked like someone that his daughter could introduce to a neighbor or even a boyfriend and not feel ashamed.

Yet, a piece of him still felt dirty. What could he do to be a father? All he could think about was his own father. *I am not getting much from my dad*, he thought. Then, he remembered the kite. He remembered the day he and his father flew the kite. That one time was all he ever learned about being a father from his father.

Henry left the bedroom. The rain had stopped. The rainbow was just about gone. The sun was continuing to shine. He could feel a breeze from the southwest beginning to kick up.

Molly was in the kitchen. She was content drinking a cup of coffee and reading the daily newspaper that had been brought to the house. The day was Saturday. Molly did not work on Saturdays.

"Molly," he said, "come with me."

She looked at him and furrowed her eyebrows. "What's up?" She gave him an uncertain smile.

"Come with me. I need to show you something."

160

So, Henry took her to his treasure well next to the apartment building. All of his belongings were there. He only cared about one belonging.

"What's this?" She asked.

"This is my secret storage locker. No fee. I keep my valuables here."

Molly looked at the well piled with different items. "Why do you continue to keep them here?"

"I can't carry them all." He hesitated. "But there is only one thing I really care about now."

"What's that?"

Henry held up his kite. The kite had gotten a little bent when he put it into the storage well. But he was sure it would still fly. "This is what I came for."

"A kite?" Molly asked.

"Not just any kite. This is our lucky kite."

"Why is it a lucky kite?"

"Because this is what I've always wanted to do with my daughter."

"We are going to fly this kite together. We should have done this when you were a little girl. We have to make up for lost time." Henry fumbled through the well, looking for the kite string. Finally, his hand felt it. When he pulled the string, two of his shirts popped out.

Molly was slightly amused at seeing the shirt. She asked, "Are those important, too?"

"Only the kite and, of course, the string." He was almost giddy because he was so excited.

He led her to the large park a few blocks from the treasure well. In the northeast corner of the park was a plateau covered with grass. The two climbed the plateau. The field at the top was large. Molly could feel the wind in her face. She was curious.

"I have never flown a kite before," she said.

"No worries. My father showed me how. Just like I am going to show you how. Just like you will show your children how." Molly was unsure what to think. She knew that she was grateful to have a father and grateful to be able to fly a kite with her father.

So, the father and daughter spent hours running with the kite across the plateau field. At first, Molly was cautious, but soon she got the hang of it, and the kite soared through the air. "You are a natural," shouted Henry over the wind.

Occasionally, an onlooker would stop to watch, but mostly they were alone.

On the way home, Molly asked, "Can we do this again?"
"Anytime you want," said Henry. For the first time, he felt like a real father.

www.ingramcontent.com/pod-product-compliance
Lightning Source LLC
Chambersburg PA
CBHW031310160726
47993CB00001B/358